The Gospel of Mammon,
and Other Odd Christian Tales

Lincoln Espy

Copyright © 2024 Lincoln Espy

Printed in the United States of America
Paperback ISBN: 978-1-64873-515-8
eBook ISBN: 978-1-64873-516-5

Publishing by Writers Publishing House
Prescott, Arizona
writerspublishinghouse.com

All rights reserved. No part of this book may be reproduced in any manner without written permission from the author except with brief quotations embodied in critical articles and reviews.

Acknowledgements

With thanks to Kara for her editing expertise
John for his encouragement
Joyce for her endurance

Cover design by Kara Nieves

Bible quotations are from the King James Version
and the Revised Standard Version

Preface

These stories were written many years ago, in my "salad days," a period of about thirty years from the mid-1970s to the late '90s. But they are rooted in the experiences of earlier years—born in Istanbul in 1952, pre-teen years in Rochester NY, young teen years as a Missionary Kid in Hong Kong, re-entry to American life in the chaotic hippie era. I did not handle these changes well. Looking back, I would say I was hyper-sensitive. I have often seemed to be out-of-step with the culture around me, and likewise with the religious environment I was in. This affected my writing.

I confess I do not write conventional stories, where events proceed to a predictable conclusion. Fiction writing is all about perspective. Consider Jesus, who was a great storyteller—the Good Samaritan, the Prodigal Son, the Lost Sheep, and 22 more. In our day his parables are the stuff of children's Sunday School lessons. But in his own time, he stirred up his hearers. Many people were mystified, some offended, but none were bored. Jesus provided a new perspective on familiar situations and events, attaching eternal meaning to them.

This is what I am after in these stories—to give a different perspective on the ordinary. If the reader is bored, or finishes a story without thinking,"Wait, what?" or "That's not what I expected," then I have missed the mark.

Contents

Acknowledgements
Preface ... i
The Middle-Aged Christian ... 1
Spelunking ... 10
The Easter Parade ... 13
The Night Shift ... 16
The Gospel of Mammon ... 21
Jericho March ... 50
Holy Rollers ... 52
A Sign of the Times ... 55
The Prodigal Brother ... 61
Black Rain ... 66
California Dreaming ... 69
Six Flags Over Jerusalem ... 74
The Cruise ... 103
Thru Hiker ... 110
Jairus' Daughter ... 119
Identity Theft ... 122
No God ... 129
Double Honor ... 137
Of Wind and Wave ... 177
Star Trek ... 182

The Middle-Aged Christian

And now I was well along on my journey on that path known to believers of all ages, that royal road that leads us out of the town of our birth and to that Heavenly City in which we have claimed our citizenship. How far along I was I cannot say, for this journey is not measured in miles or years of duration, but in gradual transformations of character—so that at journey's end, we not only find ourselves in a new place, but discover ourselves to be new people, of like nature to our fellow believers. So I cannot give you the precise distance from the old city, but I had struggled up a good many high places, trudged through numerous valleys void of light, and spent an apparent eternity in the dry country with only an occasional spring for relief. This is terrain familiar to many wayfarers. How refreshing it was, then, to enter a more pleasant environment. *This is quite a change*, I thought. *Perhaps I'm getting near the outer regions of my destination.* I began to see others heading in the same direction, and my spirit lifted as we exchanged greetings and encouragement.

And then ahead of me was a beautiful park, right beside the main path, with a great host of people gathered inside it—some resting on the grass, some walking and talking together, some singing. I turned aside and approached the entrance. The breeze carried the scent of flowers and the happy voices of those within. Would I be welcome here?

Suddenly, a man spotted me standing there uncertainly and ran up to greet me. He was a large and smiling person with a ready handshake.

"Praise God, Brother! What's your name?"

"Pilgrim," I said.

"Are you bound for God's country?"

"Why yes, sir, I am."

"That's marvelous, truly wonderful," he said exuberantly. "We've had so many people coming to us recently, and you are more than welcome to join us."

"What is this place, and who are these happy people?" I asked.

"Ah, bless you, friend; this is the Garden of First Fruits, given to us by our very own Lord and Savior Himself, for the rest and upbuilding of road-weary saints. I am the caretaker, Ernest Middle-Age by name—perhaps you've noticed the gray hairs, the bald spot...." And here he bent over so I could see for myself the state of his pate. "But I assure you that whatever I may have lost on top, I've gained around the middle, ho, ho, ho!"

I endeavored to smile at his good humor, but still felt a bit confused about where I found myself.

"I'm not sure, sir, that this is where I belong, for though I confess to being tired of the journey at times, I am yet somewhat shy of middle age."

"Ah, tut, tut, tut." And with a broad arm on my shoulder, he ushered me into the park. "You are still thinking in worldly ways. Why, we have people of many different ages here—young, and old, and in-between—but all, like yourself, have been on the road for quite a while. Now they're enjoying a foretaste of the Kingdom life, and you shall, too."

And so I put down my knapsack and guidebook and wandered around within the safe borders of the large park. My host had been correct: there were many people present, all of them recuperating from long treks through the wilderness. I found their company and conversation most congenial.

But one day I overheard a discussion among several of my new friends that troubled me. There were a half-dozen of us sitting under the spreading branches of a large shade tree. An older gentleman, Andrew Goeasy, spoke up.

"You know, I really am glad to get a break from all that traveling. Frankly, I don't care if I ever see another stretch of desert or swampland again."

"That's the nice thing about this place," said Esther Coastalong. "They never force you to move on unless you want to. There's always a welcome and a meal and warm Christian fellowship."

"And good music on Sundays," chimed in her cousin, Alma Dimlight. "Why, I've been here forty-three years and met the most wonderful people, true pillars of the church. Take Parson Dribbletruth, for instance. Such a sweet man, and what delightful sermons he comes up with."

"That's just the trouble with you all," cut in another voice abruptly. "Some of you have been here so long your roots go deeper than the trees. Why, I do believe the birds would make their nests in your hair were they not scared off by the noise of your snores!"

I turned sharply to look at the speaker; it was another newcomer to the park named John Heartfire.

Esther immediately protested. "Young man, how rude of you to say such things and disturb the bonds of Christian peace and civility that bind us all together. I know that you are new here, and inexperienced in the mature Christian life, so I shall endeavor to forgive your harsh words."

"Oh, humbug," he replied. "You act as though you're in the Heavenly City itself, instead of at one of the first resting places on the way. Look at those stringy legs—" He gave her a poke, from which she at once recoiled. "Can you even walk anymore the path we're called to follow? Do you think Jesus is going to come back here and pick you up and carry you there Himself?"

"And why not?" she replied indignantly. "If you knew more about the Christian life, you'd know that we're saved by His grace and not our works."

"He's right, you know," said a quieter voice, belonging to Ellen Gentlefaith. "It's been nice, like you said, Andrew, to be here and rest awhile. But we should be moving on to whatever lies ahead. That's what God has called us to, and we must never forget that, nor settle for anything less."

"That's easy for you to say now," put in Andrew, "but just go outside the gates a half-mile down the road, and then see how you both feel about it." Esther nodded vigorously. "There are wolves lying in wait out there. We've seen plenty of eager beavers, haven't we, ladies?" he continued. "They take a night's lodging here, and then up and off they go, without a backward glance. But just wait a bit and, lo and behold, who arrives—a week, a month, even a year later—but that same traveler. Only now he's bedraggled and disheartened. Sometimes takes quite a while to come out of it and settle in here."

"That's so true, Andrew," agreed Alma. "See, there's one of them over there." She pointed at Carl Dryhope sitting by himself a little way off. "He could have saved himself a lot of struggle if he'd just been sensible."

"Oh, and remember the old fellow," said Esther, "that guy with the beard and staff. He refused even to spend an evening here; said he didn't have the time. We never did see him again—must have died on the trail."

"He's probably sitting at Jesus' table in the Heavenly City right now," interrupted John.

"Hardly," sniffed Andrew. "He was in no shape for such a journey."

"I'll bet the wolves got him," chimed in Alma.

"The point is," said John, irritably, "there you sit all comfy and cozy, content to spend the rest of your days inside this park. You talk of faith and victory and the Christian walk, and all the while you twiddle your thumbs. Were we not all commanded to follow our Lord, wherever He led us? Don't His footsteps go on past the front gate? So who gave you permission to end your journey here? Why, I do believe there's less moss on some of the stones in this place than on the backsides of some of the residents."

"Young man," said Esther sternly. "Again, I must reprove you for your judgmental attitude. This is not a Christlike spirit."

"You make the mistake common to most fanatics and cultists," added Andrew disdainfully. "You take a few verses of Scripture and run away with them. But God asks of us only what we can give. Now Alma here has a wonderful way of keeping the hedges trimmed and tidy . . ."

"Oh, Andrew, that's such a small thing. Don't mention it further," Alma said, blushing.

"... it's her way of serving God, of glorifying Him in this place. I myself polish the doorknobs of the church each Friday. Humble duties? Yes, certainly, but who is to say that they don't in their own way build up God's Kingdom on earth?"

"Amazing!" replied John, shaking his head. "Here I thought all along we were called to a life of proclaiming the good news of Christ to dying mankind, but what I find is God's people out trimming rosebushes and polishing doorknobs. Incredible! Why the very fences around the park ensure that none of the lost and hungry could ever get in, even if they cared to."

"Now that's not so," said Alma. "They can come in the front gate, like the rest of us."

"I don't think John means to judge you," said Ellen patiently.

"Yes, I do," he interrupted morosely.

"Well, what I am concerned about," she continued, "is that we don't lose heart and cease from our labors for God's will to be done in us and in the world out there. We mustn't forget the commission Jesus gave each of us to take His gospel to a lost world. I think John is right when he says we should continue to follow our Lord down the path, regardless of the consequences."

Andrew shook his head.

John got up suddenly. "I'm off—no more flapjaw for me. Will you come, Miss Gentlefaith?"

"Yes, I will—so long as you don't go too fast. Sometimes, John, you do run on so, and I prefer a slower, more sure-footed pace."

"You're breaking fellowship, then?" said Esther coolly. "Sowing division in the body of Christ?"

John opened his mouth to react, but Ellen quickly interposed. "No, dear, just look at it as a different calling. You serve inside the gates, we go outside. There need be no hard feelings between us."

"What about you, Pilgrim?" John vented his emotion on me. "You've been silent through all of this. Will you come with us along the road to the Heavenly City, or will you sit here and develop a 'ministry' of mowing the grass or keeping the birdbaths filled with water?"

"Now, John," scolded Ellen. "Let him make up his own mind without your sarcasm."

I recoiled from his question. I dreaded it. It was so nice here, so pleasant for a change. Here was everything I had lacked back in the world. I was cared for and known by name. There was plentiful opportunity for uplifting conversation, cultivation of the mind and soul—without the dreadful incursions and disharmonies of the outer world. But when he spoke to me, I stood up and faced him and said quietly, "My name, sir, is Pilgrim, and I will be true to my name."

So we bade adieu to our companions and headed back to the main gate. Ernest Middle-Age intercepted us and entreated us not to depart so hastily. John Heartfire walked past him without a word.

"I'm afraid our minds are made up," said Ellen, and Ernest shook his head regretfully.

"Remember," he said solicitously, pressing my hand in his, "you will always be welcome here. You'll always have a place of refuge from the trials of the journey."

"Thank you," I said. Then I picked up my guidebook and knapsack where I'd left them by the gate. I turned into the road, Mr. Middle-Age seeing me to the path. John was already rounding a bend up ahead, while Ellen walked more slowly. I followed her, then turned to give the beautiful park a last wistful glance. Mr. Middle-Age had his back to me as he went inside. And as he did so, I caught a glimpse—or was it only a trick of the eyes?—of a gray tail sticking out from under his jacket, the tail of a healthy and obviously well-fed wolf.

Spelunking

My back was hurting. Some wrinkle in the rock wall pressed against my skin as I leaned back. My bottom wasn't very comfortable either, as I sat on the uneven floor. Why had I chosen such a poor place to rest?

I couldn't see anything around me—it was pitch black. It seemed I had left my lantern at home. Or maybe it had gone out. I couldn't remember. And now I became aware of a trickle of water down the wall behind me onto my right shoulder. My right arm was covered with an icky slime—what a stupid place to have sat down!

Still I sat, so very tired. I was cold, too—why hadn't I brought my coat? Surely I could have anticipated the chilly air? But by now the cold had penetrated my body, so that I could not even manage to shiver. It slowed me down, hampered my thoughts, and dulled my senses.

Occasionally, I could hear the scurrying of tiny, unseen creatures along the walls or floor, or even feel them as they passed across my body. Yet I did not brush them away. I was having difficulty remembering how I had come to this particular spot. One thing I knew: it was a vast cavern with many chambers and connecting passages. And me, fool that I was, lost somewhere in the midst of it!

But at least I was not alone; that was one blessing. I had not been stupid enough to go into the caves by myself! My companion rested beside me on my left, back against the wall, likewise staring into the void. Idly I wondered if his spot was drier than mine. We didn't speak—words would have seemed impious in that silent place—but we held hands, his right hand in my left, and I was glad for this gesture of companionship in the otherwise barren hole.

We had been sitting too long, though. His hand was as cold as the dark air. I wondered if mine felt the same to him. Now I must confess my embarrassment to you, privately: I did not even know his name. This caused me a good deal of consternation at the time, for I did not wish to offend him, and I sat there trying my best to remember his name and where we had first met. But that infernal cold kept interfering with my recollections. So I sat and he sat, each waiting for the other to speak first or make some movement to rise.

* * *

To eyes that did not see and to ears that could not hear, there came a blinding burst of light and a simultaneous inrush of sound. The cave—it was collapsing on us! No, no, the rock held firm. The light exploded in my head and the cry of a human voice echoed in my ears. I gasped as the double shock hit me, and air rushed into my collapsed lungs in a painful surge. The whole chamber was alight to my eyes for the first time. But how cramped and low it was, barely four feet high and six feet wide, with rough-hewn walls of rock and dirt. I turned my head and watched little black bugs darting away from me. I breathed in again and felt the cold leave my body and sink back into the cave walls.

My mind awoke with a start—that voice had called my name. A great feeling of relief passed over me, as I thought that a rescue party was searching for us. But this was no state to be found in, all wet and hunched over lazily against the wall. Besides, I noticed for the first time, it smelled bad in here, too.

"Come," I said, turning to my friend, "let us leave this place to go meet them." But as I lifted his hand, I saw that it had no flesh to it. And his face, it had no eyes! I jumped up in horror, dropping his arm. It clattered to the ground. Panic gripped me, and great confusion. How had I come here? I had to get out. I staggered over to the far side of the room where a beam of light entered, and there, looking upward, I could see blue sky. Stumbling up some rough steps, I plunged outside, straight into the outstretched arms of a plain but smiling man who greeted me warmly—"Lazarus . . . my friend!"

The Easter Parade

As Harry Wesner drove home from work, his thoughts turned to Jesus Christ. This was very unusual for Harry, for he could in no way be considered a religious person. Devotion was a habit gratefully shed in his mid-teen years. Since then, he had done his best to avoid all private and public displays of piety and, we must admit, he had succeeded very well. He had hurried to join the throng who, recognizing themselves not to be righteous and not wishing to become so, derided the very idea of moral earnestness and all those exhibiting it. There was no problem big enough, no question so serious, that a pitcher of Pabst could not wash it away.

Harry believed in goodness but not righteousness. Goodness was the general quality of rational men; righteousness, the unattainable standard of puritans. He believed in ethics, but not morality. Ethics was a statement of good intent; morality was the mandating of certain behavior. He believed in evil, but not sin. Evil was irrational choice; sin was the violating of those nitpicky laws that morality prescribed. He believed in the perfectibility of man and society, if only the superstitions and primitive vestiges of the past could be done away with. Harry did not believe in eternity or in heaven, but in dissolution: the slow dispersal of the molecules that constituted him into other animate and inanimate things. He did not believe even in the spiritual survival of a disembodied soul or personality—these also disintegrated to nothingness. Harry believed in God, but not that man could know anything about God. For after all, in that case He wouldn't be God, would He? Harry approved of religion, so long as it was a personal matter and not publicized.

This was Harry's credo, though he would hardly have called it that. It was nothing he would have brought together in one statement. These were just the obvious opinions that had accrued to him as he passed through life. These were the sensible notions that had stuck to him as he had gone about the real business of enjoying life.

But his beliefs are really of no consequence to us, and we must not be too hard on him if they fail to coincide with our own. We can only accuse him of failure on one count: that he did not take life seriously; that all the issues of life were subordinated to matters of lifestyle.

So now, as he drove into his driveway, it was quite unusual for him to think about Jesus, and even feel a little emotion towards Him. Harry's wife greeted him with a look of surprise and concern. "Harry, it's only 1:30. Are you ill?"

"No," he said, putting down his briefcase. A twinge of gratitude toward that long-dead man colored Harry's thoughts, as he reflected on the benefits gained for mankind by Jesus' death on the cross two thousand years ago. "It's Good Friday," he explained. "They gave us a half day off."

The Night Shift

Davis Anderson put his newspaper aside and glanced at his watch—11:15 p.m. He'd been at work an hour and fifteen minutes. Maybe the auditorium had cleared out enough by now so that he and the rest of the night crew could start cleaning up. He walked out of his basement office and up two flights of stairs to the main floor's outer corridor. A few people were slowly making their way out of the large exit doors to the street but, from the volume of sound coming from the main hall, Davis could tell the program was still going on. This bothered him—it would make it a long night for the custodial staff. They wouldn't be able to start cleanup until probably around midnight.

He walked up two more flights of stairs to one of the balconies overlooking the large floor. Carlos and Tim were there, standing on one side so they could see everything going on. He went over to them.

"Quite a show, man!" said Carlos, grinning at him.

Davis looked down. About two thousand people were gathered below them, many of them standing clustered at the front of the auditorium. A large banner over the stage proclaimed, *"Rev. Jesse Roberts Healing Crusade."* Underneath it, a Black preacher was shouting into a microphone, his words running together in an ecstatic ramble.

"In Jesus' name, they must go! Demons must flee, their power is broken—in Jesus' name! You are set free now. Receive your miracle!"

The crowd responded with shouts: "Amen!" "Yes, Lord!" A great energy moved over the people; they milled around praying, swaying, calling on God, their hands lifted high. Some were shaking, or mumbling nonsense syllables. A few were lying on the floor, where they were surrounded by people touching them and praying over them.

All over the hall it was pandemonium. The preacher's assistants moved among the crowd, praying enthusiastically over everyone they could get to, and daubing them with liquid from small bottles that they carried. On stage, a gospel band was attempting to provide background music to the spectacle before them, but was largely drowned out by noise from the people.

Davis saw a large woman standing in the middle of the room, with a half-dozen people around her who were holding her up and preventing her from collapsing on the floor. Her hands were waving above her head. She was shaking continuously, and tears streamed down her face. "Thank you, Jesus," she kept repeating. "Thank you, Jesus!"

"You shoulda been here, Dave," Tim said to him. "Some old lady in a wheelchair suddenly shot up and started running around like a bee stung her."

"Yeah, and look at that kid," Carlos pointed to a youngster thrashing around on the floor, while several adults held him down and prayed for him.

The preacher was still shouting into the microphone: "Satan, you are defeated! Leave that crippled body, leave that tormented mind, leave this room tonight, we command you in Jesus' name!"

Davis shook his head. "They're damn crazy," he muttered, and left the arena. He went back downstairs to his office.

Last week it had been a mob of screaming rich white kids in bizarre clothes who had packed the auditorium to hear the rock group Flies. He thought they were going to tear the place apart—in fact, some of the seats in Section 12 had been smashed, and the stage had been damaged when the teenagers had rushed it. It had taken two shifts to clean the hall after that one-night performance. The filth was indescribable: trash, food, clothing, vomit, even blood.

Now the same thing was going on—a different crowd, mainly Black, a lot of sick and elderly, but just the same: out of their flippin' minds. He shut the office door in disgust.

"I wonder what they've got coming in next week," he thought to himself anxiously. He looked at the auditorium schedule tacked on the bulletin board: *Annual Convention of the National Association*

of Graphic Designers. Relieved, he picked up his newspaper and sat down.

***

They finally started cleaning about 12:30 a.m. While the crusade staff disassembled the sound equipment up front, Davis and his men mopped up the balconies and rear main floor. It wasn't so bad: lots of printed programs and offering envelopes to be trashed, several Bibles and purses to go to Lost and Found. But as they neared the front of the main floor, it got worse—the chairs and floor were littered with debris.

"Hey, Dave!" Carlos called to him. "Watch this."

Tim was lolling in an abandoned wheelchair, his head to one side, eyes open and tongue sticking out. Carlos stood over him with a discarded Bible in his left hand.

"Hey, you!" he shouted at Tim. "Get up out of that wheelchair, in Jesus' name! I pronounce you healed." He laid a hand on Tim's head. "Devil, get out of this boy in the name of Jesus!"

Tim started gurgling and shaking and spitting. Carlos grabbed the chair and tipped Tim onto the floor.

"I said you're healed, sucker!"

Tim jumped up yelling, "I'm healed! I'm healed! Hallelujah! Ah, mumba, mumba, mumba, mumba! Praise you, Jesus!"

He and Carlos were laughing, but Davis was irritated.

"Aw, cut the crap. Pick up all this junk."

Before them, the seats and floor were covered with cast-off medical paraphernalia: braces, crutches, canes, walkers, hearing aids, glasses, slings, even bandages, casts, and wheelchairs. It looked like a bombed-out medical supply warehouse.

"Jesus!" Davis swore.

"What do we do with it all?" Carlos asked, dragging over the remains of a demolished sickbed.

"Stick it in Lost and Found for thirty days, I guess, then trash it."

"OK, but we'll have to open up the big storeroom to hold it all."

Davis glanced at his watch—3:15 a.m. Three more hours 'til quitting time.

The Gospel of Mammon

I

It was Thursday afternoon, right before supper, when it all started. I felt wasted—it had been a hard week at work. I was sitting in the recliner, leafing through a Christian magazine, my mind wandering. The following ad in the Classified section caught my eye:

ATTENTION SELF-STARTERS!

- Do you want to be your own boss?
- Do you want to be involved in Christian ministry?
- Do you want to enjoy a substantial income?
- Do you have $20-50,000 available to invest?

> **Did you answer 'Yes' to at least 3 out of 4 of the above questions? If so, you may qualify. Innovative Church Concepts, Inc., is seeking new investors to own and operate local franchises in select geographic areas. Ground floor opportunity in new service business. Call the 800 number for a free information packet.**

I reread the ad slowly. Be my own boss? Who wouldn't like that? Be involved in ministry? Of course, but I haven't been to seminary. A substantial income? That's a no-brainer. Twenty to fifty grand? Go fish! But still, I answered "Yes" to three of the four questions. I wondered what their angle was. There wasn't much to go on, but I was curious. What kind of a franchise would involve ministry opportunities?

"Hey, Elaine." I walked into the kitchen to show the magazine to my wife. "Look at this."

She read it briefly.

"So?" She shrugged and went back to making supper. Her lack of interest irked me.

"Well, what do you think? Doesn't it sound interesting, or at least different?"

"Nope."

She got something from the refrigerator. "Are we going to have the Andersons over on Monday or Wednesday night?"

"Wait a minute, hold on," I replied. My wife is very adept at changing our conversations from my agenda to hers. "Let's talk about the Andersons later. What's wrong with the ad?"

"It's a rip-off," she said tersely.

Elaine has always been one for quick and illogical judgments that frequently turn out to be right.

"How do you know that?" I persisted.

"I just know."

"But it's what we've talked about—our own business, extra income, helping people."

"I am not going to do phone soliciting."

I raised my voice. "It doesn't say anything about phone soliciting."

"It's always that, or junk mail." She shut the oven door decisively.

I sighed—I had seen this pattern before. So many of our conversations on Important Subjects petered out like this, deciding nothing, resolving nothing. But I wasn't willing to let this one go. I tried once again.

"Elaine," I said slowly, as if speaking to a reluctant ten-year-old, "this is different; it's a franchise of some kind. I admit we don't know anything more than that, but at least we could call for more information, couldn't we? It's a free phone number. What do we have to lose?"

"Our shirts. I think Wednesday would be better."

"Wednesday?" She'd lost me.

"To have the Andersons over."

There, she'd done it again, switched gears on me. Earlier in our marriage, I would have left it at that and slunk back to the living room, defeated. But over the years, I had learned to work the odd pattern of our communication to my occasional advantage. Now she had given me just the key I needed.

"Monday!" I shot back.

"Huh?" Now she was on the defensive.

"Monday, it's got to be Monday!" I pressed the attack.

"But, Harold," she said plaintively, "the kids have music lessons, and I've got the hairdresser's appointment…"

"Monday," I repeated. "By Wednesday, I'll be too tired."

"But I don't think I can get everything together in that short a time."

"Monday," I insisted. "And that free 800 number phone call doesn't obligate us in any way, you know."

"Oh, I don't care about that, Harold. Do what you want. But I don't think it's fair of you to demand I get everything set up by Monday."

Inwardly I gloated. Outwardly I put up a show of objecting, but at last magnanimously relented on the date of the dinner. I had managed to win her consent! To paraphrase a recent Sunday school lesson at church: if my actions were not the expression of her perfect will, at least they were within the limits of her permissive will.

I returned to the living room, quite pleased with myself, and picked up the phone.

II

Ten days later, I received in the mail a packet of sales material, consisting of an exuberant introductory letter and some glossy brochures. "Welcome to Innovative Church Concepts," the letter began, "and the opportunity of a lifetime—the chance to own your own local church outlet." It described a "revolutionary new concept" in church planting, which was to establish small, standardized "retail units" in "high-traffic corridors." It talked about market segments, product mix, quality control, return on investment. Yet, in the same paragraphs, it mentioned outreach, ministry, evangelization. The brochures displayed colorful bar graphs of income projections, per capita sales, and net decisions for Christ.

After a half-hour of thumbing through it, I was utterly bewildered. What were they selling? How can you discuss salvation and pre-tax income on the same page? I was about to put the whole packet aside when one page caught my attention. It was an artist's full-color rendering of a boxy building somewhat larger than my garage, made of plastic and glass, with a drive-up window on one side, a fenced-in children's playground out front, a green roof with a short white steeple topped by a white cross, and a large sign out front reading *"Pathways—over 50,000 saved coast to coast."*

I stared at the picture. Now at last it all started to come together, all the charts and graphs and sales hype. This picture summarized what they were talking about and proclaiming as a great event—the arrival of the church of the future.

"Elaine," I called out. Then louder: "Elaine, come look at this!"

She came hurriedly into the room.

"What's the matter, Harold?"

"Here," I said, handing her the picture.

"What is it?" she asked.

"You remember that business opportunity I called on about two weeks ago?"

"The one with phone soliciting?"

"It didn't have anything to do with phone soliciting!" I replied curtly. "It was about owning our own business."

"Oh, that one."

"Yes, that one. Well, that's it," I concluded, pointing at the picture.

She considered it a moment.

"What is it, Harold, a pizza restaurant?"

"Nope, guess again," I said smugly.

"Harold, how do I know?" She was getting flustered. "Is it a laundromat?"

"Elaine." It was my turn to get irritated. "Does that look anything like a laundromat, with a drive-up window and a playground out front?"

"Well, why not? You could drop the laundry off at the window and leave the kids in the playground, and an hour later—"

"It is *not* a laundromat, Elaine," I interrupted. "Look at the sign. It is an instant church, or, in their terms, an L.O.R.E, a Locally Owned Religious Establishment."

She was silent, shocked maybe, and studied the picture for a minute with what I hoped was mounting fascination, but which turned out to be unmistakable revulsion.

"Oh, gosh no, Harold!" she said, thrusting the picture back at me. "Not McChurch."

III

This, however, was not the end of the matter. Three days later I received a phone call from Jim Powell, who introduced himself as the regional vice president of Innovative Church Concepts. He asked if I'd received the information packet and what I thought about it.

"Well, frankly, Mr. Powell, we found it a bit confusing."

"That doesn't surprise me, Harold. It's an exciting new concept that takes some getting used to. That's why I'm calling. I would like the opportunity to meet with you and Mrs. Travers and go over the whole picture, answer any questions you might have, and discuss your future with ICC."

"ICC?"

"The abbreviation for Innovative Church Concepts, the parent company of Pathways stores."

"Oh. Well, at this point, I'm not sure that . . . I mean, my wife and I both feel that it's a great concept, but . . ."

"Now, I'll be in your area the week after next to meet with other prospective investors like yourself. It's hot, Harold, let me tell you. We're getting a phenomenal response. I can barely keep up with our expansion. Now's the time to hop aboard. By next year, exclusive territories will have been assigned and the prime units snapped up."

"It sounds very intriguing, Mr. Powell, but . . ."

"Good, now let me see, I have two openings for the week of the eighteenth. Which night would be better, Monday or Wednesday?"

The only excuse I can give for what happened next is that I was tense, under pressure, trying to think how to get myself out of this conversation. When he asked that question, it sounded so familiar that the answer just popped right out on its own.

"Monday, it's got to be Monday!"

"Monday it is," Jim agreed. "I'll look forward to seeing you and Mrs. Travers on the eighteenth at 7:30. Be sure and have all your questions ready."

He hung up. I stood there holding the phone. This was not what I had intended. I don't honestly know *what* I had intended. Like a little boy who has just ripped a hole in his new pants and has to face his mother, I went to tell Elaine. She was most unsympathetic.

"Harold, when will you learn to say 'No' to people? You've got to stop being so nice to everybody."

I apologized, sarcastically, for being a nice person. She ignored that and asked me if she hadn't told me in the first place that it was a bad idea. I admitted she had, then went out on the porch to sulk. Later, she came out with a glass of iced tea for me.

"It's all right, Harold. It'll work out." She sounded like she meant it.

"I sure hope so."

"Yes, it will. Everyone's entitled to screw up once in a while."

"Thanks," I said sourly.

Over the next several days, I alternated between wild hopes of a new calling in life and the cynical realism my wife expressed. Was it really possible for laypeople to be involved in Christian ministry? Could I serve God full-time without having to live below the poverty line? Could one build a bridge between business and Christian service? Probably not; probably it would turn out to be just a pyramid marketing scheme to sell some brand of Christian cosmetics. But at least I was going to find out.

IV

By Monday evening, I was pretty wound up. I came home from the office early to make sure the house was clean. I re-vacuumed the living room, much to Elaine's annoyance.

"You'd think Pastor Everett was coming," she said.

"There is someone here greater than Pastor Everett," I replied tensely. Then, in alarm, "Why didn't you dust the corners?" I removed a small spider web from behind the front door.

"Oh, come off it, Harold."

"I just don't want to miss God, Elaine."

"We'll miss God because I overlooked a spot?"

"No, but I don't want to give a bad impression. Don't you understand how important this could be to us, to the kids, to our future and our hopes of ministry?"

"Not really," she said, shaking her head.

I sighed, then panicked. "Oh my gosh!" I exclaimed. "I forgot to shine my shoes." I ran into the bedroom.

A couple of minutes later the doorbell rang. Elaine answered it.

"Harold," she called, "the man from Amway's here."

I could have killed her! By the time I got to the living room, she had steered him to the couch and was offering him something to drink. He stood up to greet me.

"Jim Powell."

"Harold Travers."

"Good to meet you, Harold."

Jim was in his late forties, all spit and polish, three-piece suit, briefcase, and Bible. He looked like a combination of clergyman and insurance salesman, yet I was also reminded of the guy who had tried to convince us to stockpile dehydrated foods during the Y2K scare.

Elaine came in with the coffee and we chit-chatted for a few minutes. Then Jim shifted into drive.

"Mr. and Mrs. Travers, I know you've read our introductory packet, and I'm sure you have several questions to ask. But first, I'd like to give you the history of our company and our founder, Mr. Harlan Kroc."

Jim then told us how Mr. Kroc was a successful businessman and owner of a national chain of specialty food restaurants called Food Fetish Fine Dining. Now in his late sixties, he was a multi-millionaire enjoying the fruits of financial success. At the same time, Mr. Kroc had been a long-time churchgoer and committed Christian who felt frustrated at the lack of impact of the church in the world. Concerned over the moral decline of America and the loss of the church's influence in government and community life, he had participated in, and contributed heavily to, a number of church-sponsored outreach programs. Though launched with a lot of enthusiasm and fanfare, they had all fizzled within a few months.

Mr. Kroc realized that just doing more of the same—more campaigns, larger budgets, more hoopla—wasn't going to work. Instead, an innovative approach would be necessary for Christianity to have an impact on our society. The problem, he felt, was not the Word of God or the message of salvation itself, but the delivery of that gospel to people.

Elaine interrupted. "Everybody says that, from TV evangelists to Christian rockstars."

"True," Jim responded, "but Harlan's response was unique in that he drew his solution directly from the business world in which he'd already proven his concepts successful. The entire plan of Innovative Church Concepts, the parent organization of Pathways outlets, is derived from the history of the expansion of the Food Fetish franchise network."

"What plan is that?" I asked.

Jim replied, "Mr. Kroc's vision is nothing less than the planting of a standardized unit for the proclamation of the gospel in every major population center in the nation."

"That's nothing new," Elaine interrupted again. "The Baptists have been doing that for years."

"Elaine!" I protested, but Jim cut me off.

"No, no, she's right, but with one major difference; the Baptists are mission focused, we are market focused."

Elaine frowned. "I don't get it."

"Let me give you an example," Jim said. "Suppose it's Sunday afternoon and you are out working in the yard. You look down the street and see some well-dressed people carrying Bibles going door to door. What do you do?"

Elaine got that pit bull look in her eyes.

"I get my Bible ready and wait for them on the porch steps," she said. "They could be Moonies."

"And you, Harold?"

"Oh, well, I'd probably go inside and watch TV in the basement until they're gone."

"OK," said Jim, "and what would you do if you were not a Christian?"

"Let the dog out?" I asked, not seeing what this had to do with missions and markets.

"Exactly," replied Jim. "See? All three responses you gave me were the anticipation of a threat. And the difficulty of a mission focus is that it has to overcome this barrier of mistrust and suspicion in every single contact it makes, convert by convert. And there is always the risk that, for each 'sale' made, you alienate three or four other prospects. This is what Harlan deemed the fatal flaw of a mission focus."

"So what about the other one, whatever you called it?" Elaine asked.

"A market focus. Take another example. You get some coupons in the mail offering fifty cents off McDonald's Quarter Pounders. What do you do?"

"That's simple," I said. "Within forty-eight hours we're visiting the Golden Arches."

"And," Jim emphasized, "spending another fifteen to twenty dollars to redeem those fifty-cent coupons, right?"

We nodded.

"That is market focus." He sat back triumphantly.

I didn't get it. What had this got to do with Harlan Kroc and a new plan for the evangelization of America? Elaine was quicker than I was.

"You send out coupons to go to church?" she asked, bewildered.

Jim smiled and opened his briefcase, placing several items before us. "Coupons, senior citizen discounts, ladies' nights, and children's collectible toys. We use them all, and more."

I looked at the items on the table: several brightly colored coupons with offers such as, "One dollar off one Quiet Time Combo (doughnut—coffee or juice—daily Scripture verse)" or, "Buy one afternoon Supersnack (soft drink—chips or cookies—Bible study session) at regular price, get second one free." There was also a little plastic mound among the papers. Curious, I picked it up. "Too light to be a paperweight," I said to Elaine.

"Touch that lever there," Jim said.

As I did so, one side opened up and a little figure hidden inside sprang out. I re-cocked it and tried again.

"That's Lazarus coming out of the tomb," Jim said, "one of the toys in the Bible Events series. You order a Junior Snack and it comes free."

"You're kidding."

"Nope, and don't let your kids see it. They'll kill for it. In our test market in Cincinnati, the entire stock sold out in three days."

"You mean this stuff really works?" Elaine asked incredulously.

"Of course," said Jim, "that's the whole point. Instead of you beating down their door to make the pitch, they're beating down your door and paying you to hear it. And they're not all believers either. We get tons of folks who want to get right with God but can't stand church. They're our bread and butter. Now I'd like to go over these charts with you, showing our five year plan and expansion overseas...."

"Wait a minute, hold on!" Elaine stopped him. "I am totally confused. What are you really selling?"

Jim smoothly switched gears. "OK, let's look at the Pathways product line, and that will make it clearer to you. Our big morning money-maker is the Q.T. Combo for two ninety-nine, the one on the coupon there. This gives the customer a choice of coffee or juice, a doughnut, and the Bible verse for the day printed on the doughnut wrapper. Millions of Americans are absolutely convinced that they should start the day with some kind of devotional. It has been drilled into them by their churches. And we appreciate that because, while the churches foster the need, they aren't able to fulfill it. For example, you, Harold, how many days a week do you actually manage to spend ten minutes in prayer and Bible-reading before work?"

"Um, well, maybe . . ."

"See, Harold, I told you," Elaine cut in. "If you'd just set the alarm for 6:00 a.m. instead of 6:15, you wouldn't have to apologize."

"But that's the point," Jim defended me. "Nearly everybody is the same way. So you have all these people out there with a constant sense of guilt—presto, a ready market for us to reach. On the way to work, or after leaving the kids at school, they can drop by their local Pathways outlet and in five minutes take care of their daily obligation. We give them the mini breakfast, the Bible verse and prayer starter, a loaner Bible if needed, inspirational music in the background, and a comfy environment for sitting and reading and saying a prayer. They give us their guilt and two dollars and ninety-nine cents. And as you can see from this table here, our net is one dollar eighty cents per unit sale, which compares favorably with the return on hamburgers at those other franchises. And for those who are really rushed, the Combo is packaged for takeout or drive-thru; they can gulp the coffee, glance at the Bible verse, and pray while stuck in bumper-to-bumper traffic."

"You mean people really do that?" I asked.

"Of course," Jim replied. "Maybe you should, too. But that is just the kickoff. Around 9:00 a.m. we switch over to Morning Coffee Time. This is geared to a declining market segment of stay-at-home mothers. But fast food places normally have a decline until the lunch crowd starts coming in around 11:30, and we've found this a lucrative way to plug that gap. We offer these women hour-long get-togethers and social times around a biblical topic. This is a longer version of the Quiet Time product. Many of them order the Combo and then join the group, which is more profitable for us. Also, it means that both husband and wife are covering the same ground in their devotions, which enhances their communication and reinforces the incentive to make us part of their daily routine. That repeat business is very important to us. Anyway, the light Bible study/sharing times start every half hour through 11:00, and women attend the same group each day. And what is the greatest concern of all these mothers?" He turned to my wife.

"The laundry?" Elaine asked.

"What to do with their preschool children," Jim corrected her. "And that's what the fenced-in play area is for. We provide supervision for the kids, so the mothers get a midmorning break to get with God and other mothers. We also provide a group leader, called a hostess, a bottomless coffee pot, the daily theme, and a friendly atmosphere. We have an extremely loyal clientele with this product. Some mothers have told us it's the main thing that has helped them to keep their sanity."

"Hey, I'd sign up," Elaine agreed. "But what happens at lunch, Bible burgers?"

"Oh no, we don't sell lunches, per se. We offer the environment in which to eat lunch. From 11:30 to 1:30 is our heaviest volume. We expect people to bring a sack lunch from home or buy a takeout from a fast food place, then bring it to Pathways to eat it. We avoid the problems of hot food preparation and concentrate on the high-profit sidelines—beverages, chips. We offer three separate lunchtime product lines for busy people: Lunch and Pray, Lunch and Share, Lunch and Study. They're all similar to the Morning Coffee format—one-hour small groups led by a host or hostess. The prayer slot is for people who want a heavier prayer dose than afforded by the Q.T. morning special. The share time is for talkers, people who like to discuss current events from a spiritual perspective. The topic for the week is set in advance by ICC headquarters. A host moderates the group, makes sure everyone is involved, no one dominates, and nothing too heavy goes on. Keeping it light and fast-paced is essential. And the third track is Bible study, our most popular lunchtime offering. Scores of office workers bring their own Bibles and regularly attend a lunchtime Bible study, again led by a host following a preset curriculum."

"Sure, I'd try it," I agreed, "but what if I wanted to study Hebrews and you only offered Psalms?"

"We make sure we have a good mix going all the time—an Old Testament offering, a New Testament one, and some topicals—Bible survey, for example, or Great Women of the Bible. But, and this is the critical thing, as with all our product lines, the courses are the same coast to coast. A businessman in Los Angeles may study Hebrews 3 on Wednesday, then fly to Atlanta on Thursday. If he goes to lunch at the Atlanta Pathways, he's guaranteed to find them covering Hebrews 4 that day—absolute certainty. It's part of our quality control procedures, which we're very committed to."

"How much do these lunchtime groups cost?" I asked.

"$4.50, minus discounts to regulars. Sales of supplementary food items boost the per capita gross to $6.75. And with total sales on these three lines alone averaging a hundred twenty-two units per day, you can see our lunchtime gross is about $825. Not great, but a good start. As you can see from this graph, with more advertising, we project annual growth rates of seventeen percent in these products."

"I guess I'm getting the picture," Elaine said. "And for supper, more of the same?"

"Oh, we have several other products, and we are constantly test marketing new ones. A big hit is our after-school Cookies and Christ program, kind of an alternative to latchkey or daycare. We supervise the kids, give them a snack and a Sunday school lesson until the parents pick them up after work. Quite lucrative products, because parents want to place their children in a trustworthy facility. That's another market niche we just stepped into. Plus, there are evening Bible studies, midweek services, and of course our famous trademark Come-As-You-Are Sunday worship services."

"How does that differ from regular church, apart from dress?"

"Our Sunday service is the result of careful research and strategic planning. We developed a generic church format that makes the service more comfortable and dilutes the spiritual heaviness of the traditional church."

"Sounds like Robert Schuller and the Crystal Cathedral," said Elaine.

"Sure, he was one of the pioneers. We're just carrying that approach to its logical conclusion. We run six morning services back-to-back, plus three evening ones, each forty-five minutes long. We sing a few songs, have a prayer and a ten minute message, then a fellowship time with free coffee and doughnuts, and a children's Sunday School lesson: all for seven dollars a head, three for kids. A great value, even better on Easter, with our spring special: 'Children free with paid adult admission.'"

"Wait just a minute, here!" I was upset. "You charge people to go to church?"

"Of course," Jim replied nonchalantly. "You have to change your way of thinking from religion to business. We charge, and people feel good about paying, especially if we send them a coupon first that makes them think we're giving them a great deal. Besides, it's a lot more upfront and honest than passing a collection plate. Do you know that our research shows that the number one negative impression of churches held by non-churchgoers is not the sense of boredom—that's number two—but the passing of the plate? It's another barrier mission focused organizations put up between themselves and the people they're trying to reach; it creates guilt in people who don't give much, and regret in people who do."

"But charging people to go to church?" I still couldn't swallow it.

"It's part of the psychology of marketing. The reason Americans ignore the gospel message is that it costs them nothing, therefore they figure it can't be worth much. If you start charging them to hear it, they'll start to listen. People really don't mind paying for things. In fact, they'll eagerly pay for things that have value to them. Then, if you give them a discount off the list price, they'll buy all they can get. It's really a great tool for evangelism. We had one offer that gave twenty percent off regular admission for the host family, and fifty percent off for their guests. It was a good promo, brought in a lot of new people.

"But let me ask you something," Jim continued. "Have you ever gone door to door on a neighborhood outreach campaign, inviting people to your church?"

"I did once," Elaine said. "Harold stayed home."

"In the basement, right?" Jim smiled. "And how did it turn out?"

"Not all that great. Maybe five families responded, but none of those I visited."

"That's a pretty good response rate for that kind of campaign. But in one test we conducted last year in Syracuse, we distributed a thousand discount coupons to homes around our unit there during the week. On the following Sunday, sixty-five families showed up with those coupons, and fifteen more the Sunday after that—an absolutely phenomenal response rate by direct-mail standards. And each of them was a paying customer."

"But aren't you competing with regular churches, drawing away their people?" Elaine objected.

"Certainly, but that's the way it is today anyway—every church is in competition with every other one. We are the aggressive newcomer, hoping to gain a significant part of the market. But—and this is the crucial difference—we are also expanding the pie by reaching all those non-churchgoers who would never go to a regular service. Yet there is a sense in which we are not in competition with other churches, just as McDonald's doesn't directly compete with Steak & Ale. If you want serious food, you don't go to McDonald's; if you want serious church, you don't come to us. We are pitching our products to the great American mainstream, which wants neither. That is why we are confident of our success."

He paused while I pondered his last remarks. They made me vaguely uncomfortable.

"You know, one thing that occurs to me," I mentioned, "is that neither my wife nor myself has any seminary training."

"I do too," Elaine reminded me. "I have a year of Bible school."

"Yes," I replied, "but that was fourteen years ago, and I don't think that counts for much now."

"I'm glad you brought that up," Jim responded. "Actually, we are far more interested in your credit rating than your theological training. People with formal training in religion are disqualified from being franchisees of ICC."

"But why?" asked Elaine.

"A matter of policy—they make very poor businessmen. You must never forget our perspective: we sell a mainstream product to mainstream America. Religious training and ordination are just obstacles in the way of getting the product, or the message, out. Aren't you somewhat intimidated by your pastor and board of elders?"

"Well, they're very nice people," Elaine said defensively.

"No doubt, but they're not normal people. Anyone who knows biblical Greek is not normal people. And the foundation of our company is that it takes Joe Average American to reach Joe Average American. So we have no place for religious professionals. Besides that, they and we have a different bottom line."

"Aren't you both working to get people saved?" I asked.

Jim sighed. "*Their* bottom line is souls; *ours* is dollars. Souls are just the byproduct of a successful business enterprise."

"Now that's what I don't like," Elaine protested. "Doesn't it say somewhere in the New Testament that you can't serve God and mammon? And it sounds to me like you guys are trying to do both."

Jim nodded. "Very perceptive, Mrs. Travers. Yes, that's in Matthew 6."

He opened his Bible and read the passage:

No one can serve two masters: for either he will hate the one and love the other, or he will be devoted to the one and despise the other. You cannot serve God and mammon (Mt 6:24 RSV).

"It is the understanding of this Scripture that is the key to understanding our company philosophy, and indeed, I believe, to undertaking a successful evangelistic enterprise in this country. Permit me...." Jim paused and took a quarter from his pocket.

"Whose picture is on this coin?" he asked.

"Caesar's," I replied lightly.

"Cute, Harold," said Elaine. "How about George Washington's?"

"And what does it say beside him?" Jim continued.

"In God we trust," I read.

"There you have it," he said, pocketing the coin.

"There you have what?" asked Elaine.

Leaning forward, Jim said very deliberately, "This country was founded on the premise that you *can* serve God and money; it grew strong and powerful on that same conviction, and the only way to restore it and get it back on its feet is to recover that basic truth. This is the philosophy of our founder, Mr. Kroc—that a successful revival in this nation must address both poles of the magnet, God *and* money. Any religious movement that omits a positive appreciation of money cannot possibly succeed in this country, because it denies a major component of our history and identity as Americans."

He sat back and took a sip of his coffee, watching our reactions to his statement.

"But you're saying the Word of God isn't true," Elaine protested.

Jim smiled. "You're good," he said, "exactly the tough-minded person we like to deal with. Look." He opened his Bible to 1 Corinthians 11:5 and read,

> Any woman who prays or prophesies with her head unveiled dishonors her head....(RSV)

"Do you wear hats to church, Mrs. Travers?"

"Not anymore; only on Easter."

"Do women ever speak in your church?"

"Of course, and the pastor's wife teaches a Sunday school class that includes men. Everybody knows that Paul was just upholding the customs of the day."

"Exactly. And the same is true, I believe, of Jesus' sayings in Matthew. In Bible times, in first-century Palestine, in the context in which it was spoken, it was absolutely correct. It was right for its time and place. But those words fit twenty-first-century Americans no better than does Paul's command on head coverings for women. And the major mistake of unsuccessful evangelistic enterprises in this country is that they've tried to apply Jesus' words in a different time and place, and ended up losing both their hearers and their impact. On the other hand, you now have the opportunity, through owning a Pathways franchise, of succeeding where they failed, of bringing God's Word to Americans in a way they can both understand and accept."

I shifted uncomfortably in my chair.

Jim stood up. "I'm going to leave you with some more literature, and an application for owning a franchise. I'd like you to consider being my guest for a tour of an operational unit. Also, here is my phone number for any questions you might have. I'll be getting back to you in a couple of weeks, but feel free to call me sooner."

"You've given us a lot to think about," I fumbled.

"—and pray about," Elaine added emphatically.

"Good," Jim nodded, "but be sure to talk to your financial advisor as well."

We walked him to the door and shook hands.

"Remember," he said, looking at me intently, "markets will win out over missions every time."

Jericho March

A man was going down from Jerusalem to Jericho. As he was about to leave, a priest came up to him and said, "It's rather late in the day to be starting out. Wouldn't it be more prudent to get an early start tomorrow morning?"

But the man replied, "Sir, if I go now, I can reach Jericho before the other merchants and get a better location in the market."

A Samaritan tradesman overheard him and offered, "Say, if you can wait a day, let us go together. It will be safer that way." But the man, being a good Jew, did not reply, or even look at him.

Then a Levite came up. "You had better spend the night inside the city walls," he warned. "There have been reports of robbers out on the road. Soon the soldiers will be sent out to make sure it's safe. I'm going to Jericho myself, but not until they've cleared the way."

The merchant shrugged and said, "Robbers!—always there are rumors of thieves on this road or that. If I listened to all the rumors, I'd still be home in bed in my mother's house with the covers over my head."

And so he set out, against their advice. He had not gone far before he fell among robbers, who stripped him and beat him, leaving him half dead.

The next day the priest was walking down that road. But when he saw the injured man, he passed by on the other side, thinking, "It serves you right. You ignored my good counsel and suffered the fate of the foolish. God is just." In the same way, the Levite also came by and went over and looked at the man. "Well, well, who have we here? Is it not Mr. Know-It-All? Thought you could get a jump on the rest of us, eh? And look how you ended up. God has judged you for your arrogance—blessed be His name." And he turned and walked away.

But when the Samaritan came to him, he had compassion and went to him and bound up his wounds, pouring on oil and wine; then he set him on his own beast and brought him to an inn, and looked after him. And the next day he took out two denarii and gave them to the innkeeper, saying, "Take care of him, and whatever more you spend, I will repay you when I come back."

The Levite was staying at the same inn and overheard the Samaritan's instructions to the innkeeper. "Truly," he said, "these Samaritans have no knowledge of God." The innkeeper nodded and pocketed the coins.

Holy Rollers

I walked into the gambling hall,
Figured for once I'd give it my all.
Went to the man who held the dice;
Said, "I'm putting my money on Jesus Christ."

The old-timers there just laughed at me
And the croupier's eyes lit up with glee.
He said, "I'll be glad to take your money, Son,
'Cause the odds on that run a hundred to one."

I put down my little stack of chips
And the gambling man took a couple sips.
Then he shot the dice across the board
And as the numbers settled he cried, "O Lord!"

For I'd won my bet as they all could see
And he pushed a mountain of chips toward me.
"Go on," he said, "and cash 'em in.
I never thought I'd see you win."

They thought that I would leave right then,
That I wouldn't be a fool and try again.
But I looked him in the eye and held my post:
"It's double or nothing on the Holy Ghost."

The smoke-filled room grew very still;
All eyes were on the sharp-eyed shill.
Cool and calm he appeared to be
'Cause he thought he now had the best of me.

Across the table the dice were thrown.
The cocktail girl let out a groan.

The Spirit fell as a mighty wind,
That room was shaking in its sin.

Now I had me the Lord and I had the Spirit
And I wasn't afraid to tell all who would hear it.
The gambler filled the board with my winnings;
He thought it was over but I was just beginning.

"I think it's time you left," he said;
"Push your luck and you could end up dead."
"I got one more bet," I said with a nod;
"I'm betting my wad on the Kingdom of God."

Well, he got on the phone to the man downstairs.
The bargirls started saying their prayers.
He wanted to know could they cover the bet;
Surely I couldn't win a third time yet!

When he got off the phone his knees were knockin':
It was all or nothing and the joint was rocking.
For when the Kingdom comes, nothing else can stand
And this place was built on shifting sand.

"We gotta take the bet, we got no choice,"
Now he was speaking in a trembling voice.
Some of the folks didn't wait to hear more:
They started heading for the door.

But I'm tired of playing religion games,
Of half-hearted commitment and hidden shames.
"I'm living God's way or not at all,"
I said to the man in the gambling hall.

Now he glared at me across the battlefield,
Each one seeing if the other would yield.

Enemies locked in a mortal fight—
Sword of the Spirit against the power of night.

One last time the dice were cast
And suddenly the whole scene passed.
I found myself in a different place
In front of a man with a radiant face.

He said, "It isn't because of your ability,
But because your heart was set on Me."
He paused to unlock two massive doors:
"Because you wagered all, the Kingdom's yours."

A Sign of the Times

The small boy was sitting by the roadside near the entrance to the marketplace. His begging bowl was in front of him, and his crutch was displayed prominently on his lap. Only two copper coins lay in his bowl, but six more were hidden in his pocket. He had learned that a beggar cannot afford to appear successful. The generosity of his patrons lessened as his bowl filled up with coins. So he kept it nearly empty.

It was late morning. Soon the midday crowd would be coming along. They would provide his main income for the day. He picked at a scab on his leg, trying to get it to bleed a little. The idea was to make it look repulsive enough to arouse sympathy in people without causing him any great pain or infection.

He had been a beggar for three years and had learned his trade well. It was a point of pride with him. Unlike the riffraff who merely pretended to be crippled, he really was lame in one leg. It's true that this leg had been purposely broken by his father, but that wasn't his own fault. It's just that he had been the smallest and thinnest of the four children, and had large eyes. From a begging standpoint, he was a "natural." So his father had contacted one of the local begging guilds, enrolled him for a fee, and broken his leg to give him a limp. The beggars' union got him a location, trained him in the rudiments of the trade, and took twenty-five percent of all he made. The territory they started him on, far out along the main road outside the city gate, wasn't a prime site, but he'd practiced his skills and bided his time. Advancement came readily; as older beggars sickened and died, he moved up the seniority list and transferred to better locations. Now he was nearly into the market area itself. Another five years and he might even make it to the Temple steps.

He heard people coming down the street and looked up. It was too early for the noon rush, so perhaps it was a troop of soldiers or some travelers arriving from out of town. In this business, it paid to be alert. Soldiers were dangerous. They would walk over you or knock you out of the way with a spear handle. Merchant caravans were a waste of time; they ignored appeals for alms. The best prospects were groups of religious pilgrims, if handled properly. By crying out for help in God's Name, one could eat well for a week off their donations.

This crowd coming toward him was obviously neither soldiers nor merchants. It was a chaotic, noisy mob of people, all milling around trying to get closer to someone in the center. The boy stood up to see better.

"What's going on?" he asked another spectator.

"It's that prophet, Jesus of Nazareth," he replied. "He's just arrived in Jerusalem on his way to the Temple. Now we ought to see some action."

The prophet Jesus—the boy had heard of him, of course. Who hadn't? A great teacher and miracle worker. Some expected him to lead the fight against Rome. Maybe that's why he had come to Jerusalem.

The boy's mind moved quickly—a beggar learns to seize his opportunities. This was not a good time to work the crowd; people were too intent on getting a look at the teacher to pay attention to him. But maybe there was another angle. Suppose he could get to the man himself? He already had reason to be grateful to the prophet: two members of the beggars' guild who were senior to him, a blind man and a deaf and dumb boy, had been healed by Jesus. That had freed up their begging stations, allowing him to move up the line. But now there was a chance that Jesus could do something else for him, something a lot more personal. He emptied his begging bowl into his pocket, set it down and picked up a scrap of discarded rag. Then he barreled into the swirl of people in front of him.

Timid beggars die young. So although the boy was small and lame, he was also agile and aggressive. He pushed through the outer wall of the crowd, wormed through a tangle of moving bodies. A large man stepped on his good foot and he winced in pain.

"Pig!" he spluttered, and stuck his crutch between the man's legs, tripping him up. As the man yelled and fell, the boy darted in closer to the middle of the pack.

Now he could see the rabbi everyone was following: a strong man, plainly dressed, moving with difficulty through the press, his eyes scanning the faces of those before him. Around him was a bodyguard of even rougher men. *"Hicks,"* the boy thought contemptuously, poor prospects indeed for either a donation or a revolution. He knew he had to penetrate this protective cordon to get to the rabbi himself.

"Jesus, Master!" he yelled, but his voice didn't carry over the noise. He worked his way up to one of the men in the inner ring and tried to duck under his arm.

"Keep back!" the man said gruffly. Ignoring him, the boy waved his arm and shouted in a high voice, "Jesus, Master, please!" He lunged against the restraining human barrier. The big man stumbled.

Whether it was his calling out, or his pushing, or the man's misstep, Jesus turned to look in the boy's direction. He knew that Jesus saw him, and not just as a body in the mass. Those eyes locked on his with interest and interrogated him.

This was what the boy had been trained for. Years of studying people and practicing his pitch had prepared him for this encounter. There was a distinctive methodology in begging that he had been well apprenticed in. Step one was to get the full attention of the target. This had now been achieved. Step two was to convey in an instant one's sense of utter helplessness and desperation in a way that would evoke sympathy. The greater the feeling stirred, the greater the contribution elicited. The boy had learned to use his crutch, his rags, his voice, his scabs, and especially his large, sorrowful eyes in a concentrated attempt to overpower the emotional defenses of his prospects. This was what he now turned on the prophet.

"Please help!" he cried out again, reaching out his hand while allowing himself to fall under the feet of the clumsy bodyguard. This forced the man to stop, while the other disciples tried to hold back the crowd. The first man picked up the boy roughly, to save him from being trampled. He hung limply in the man's arms, but kept his eyes on Jesus.

It was now time to move to step three, the Invocation of the Divine Name: "In the Name of God Most High, have pity!" This was standard procedure for all religious prospects, and ought to work doubly well with a rabbi. If it didn't produce results, step four was to yell curses at their retreating backs.

Now, however, there was no need for steps three or four, because Jesus himself had stopped. He indicated for his followers to wait, then spoke to the man holding the boy: "Bring him to me." The man pushed him forward so that he was face to face with the prophet of Galilee. The crowd pressed against them but stood quietly now, watching eagerly to see what sign Jesus would perform. The boy stood on his own, boldly looking up at Jesus. This man, too, had expressive eyes, he thought. He would have made a first-rate beggar.

"What is it that you want me to do for you?"

The boy breathed deeply, and looked briefly at the faces of the crowd framing the one face that mattered. He'd done it, he'd actually gotten through. It was time to make the pitch.

He gulped and stuck out his hand, clutching the rag he'd picked up off the street.

"Please, sir, can I have your autograph?"

The Prodigal Brother

... and he arose and came to his father. But while he was yet at a distance, his brother saw him in the road and ran to meet him, lest his father see him first.

The young man fell down at his feet, but the elder brother said disdainfully, "So the mighty adventurer returns, in splendor and glory, with riches untold!"

"Please, Brother," cried the younger man, "hear me out. I have sinned against heaven and against our father. I am no longer..."

"Don't call me 'brother'!" the older man interrupted. "The day you walked out the door you ceased to be one of the family. You have no part in us."

"I know that," he replied. "I know I can't go back to what I had before. I have not come back as a son and heir, but as a servant to you and our father."

"A servant? I wouldn't take you back as a stable boy. How dare you come to us in this condition! Look at yourself—a filthy, mangy dog. And you intended my father to see you like this? The shock would kill him!"

"No, Brother, I don't want him to see me. I don't want to cause him any further grief. But if you will go to him on my behalf, he won't even have to look at me. If you ask him, he might be willing to let me be a field hand in the farthest corner of the farm, where neither he nor yourself will notice me."

"I don't believe my ears! You've always got some angle, don't you? After what you did, squandering the fruit of his labor, not yours, bringing shame on his name and mine—you have the insolence to come back and ask us for more favors? Are you mad as well as stupid?"

The younger brother didn't reply. The older man was irate.

"You're dog meat around here, fella! I told him before you left that this would happen. 'Father,' I said, 'don't trust him with your possessions. He is a lazy and worthless fellow, and will come to ruin.' But he didn't listen to me. And all of it has been wasted, just as I feared."

The younger man cried out in desperation, "I am sorry that I lost all he gave me. I can't undo that. But now, if you send me away, I'll die. I have no one else to turn to, nowhere else to go."

"Now you ask me for help. But where were you when I was out working in the fields? Lying around the house daydreaming and playing that silly flute. And when I was up late at night going over the account books, you were out partying with your friends. Did you ever listen to me then? Did you ever get serious about life? Did you ever grow up, like I told you? No, you were having too much fun. And when I told you that you were useless, you laughed at me, you called me a butthead."

The younger man said nothing.

"So now you come to ask me to do something for you. But it is far too late for that. I cannot do anything for you. Your life is just the inevitable outcome of your irresponsible behavior. You sowed your wild oats, and now you are reaping the result."

The younger brother stood up and brushed himself off, wiping his grimy face with his sleeve.

"Well, if you won't go ask Father on my behalf, I'll go to him myself. He can't do anything worse than refuse to see me and send me away."

"Is that so? Listen, you fool, if you think I'm being rough on you, just wait 'til our father finds out what you've done. Do you think I am heartless and cruel to tell you the truth? No, it's for your own good that I am warning you not to bother him. For if he truly realized the state you are in and saw the frittering away of his possessions, of the trust he put in your hands, he would be consumed with anger. I have no doubt that he would have you publicly stoned to death, with himself throwing the first stone. Can you deny it?"

His brother did not reply. He stood looking down at the sores on his feet. He knew his brother was right because he remembered the stern discipline of his father, his own rebellion, and their frequent arguments. His brother was right: he was stupid to have left home, but crazy to have returned.

The elder brother spoke again. "Here," he said, tossing three gold coins in the dirt at his feet. "These will get you back to the city and even pay the rent for a couple of weeks. Now, can you say I am without compassion, or that I've treated you unjustly?"

The younger man shook his head.

"Good then, take them and go. Go back to the life you have freely chosen for yourself, good or ill. And never again trouble us by coming back. We want to see or hear nothing more from you."

The younger brother bent to pick up the coins, but stopped suddenly. He straightened up, looked his brother in the eye, turned, and started to walk away.

"Cain!" A voice behind them cried out, near the house. "Cain, is there anything wrong? I saw you drop something."

Both men turned, startled. An old man was coming towards them. The younger brother drew back. The elder brother, panic-stricken, thought quickly.

"No, Father, nothing is wrong, nothing at all."

"Who is that with you, my son? Does someone need food?"

The elder brother replied, "No, Father, it is your son, the one you have long wept over. See, I have searched far and wide for him, and now I have brought him to you."

The father exclaimed, "My dear son? Is it truly him, the one who was dead?"

The younger brother stared open-mouthed, first at his father, then at his brother.

The fatted calf bawled.

Black Rain

And they brought before him a man who had been crippled from his youth. He could neither walk nor stand, but only sit and drag himself along. The teacher placed his hands on the man's shoulders and asked him, "Do you believe?"

And he looked up at him and replied, "Sometimes."

The teacher commanded, "Rise and walk."

And immediately the sewers and gutters opened up, and their inhabitants rushed forth, lest he stand. They threw themselves upon the man in a great pile, so that by their weight they might keep him down. They climbed on his lap to press upon him, and mounted his back and shoulders. They entered into his ears that he might not hear the word that went forth, and into his eyes that he might not see the One who spoke. They began a great din and commotion in his mind, so that he would not comprehend the word. They sang a loud song to distract him:

> Little man, half a man,
> You are one of us.
> Let us lift and carry you
> Back into the dust.

And he would have sat down again. But it was too late; the word had been spoken. It was not a suggestion, it was not an idea, it was not a wise saying to meditate upon later as he sat in the gutter. It was a command, like that other word that brought light forth out of darkness. It was like the word that brought his people out of bondage more than a thousand years before. And there was no power in all heaven or earth that could pretend that that word had not been spoken.

So he stood up, and hesitantly took two steps. His legs looked the same, but, where before there was weakness, now there was power. One moment absolute uselessness, the next full strength. Just as one moment there was all darkness, then look—a light shining and beating back the void; or again, one day a race of slaves and the next a free people, a new nation. He took several more steps, his confidence growing.

The crowd cheered to see the miracle. "That's amazing!" exclaimed the butcher. "I've known him all my life and never seen him walk."

"That's right," the stonemason's wife added. "Now maybe he can get a job and support hisself like normal folk."

And their wonder was right. But they failed to see what the One who spoke the word saw. For as the crippled man stood up, a great black rain commenced around him, ugly black drops striking the earth with violence. They came not from the sky above, but from the sick man's body—a vast heap of sewer dwellers that had piled themselves upon him. When he stood, they lost their hold and fell cursing and kicking into the dirt. As powerless as ants in the path of an avalanche, they were dashed to the ground, whereupon they scrambled back into their holes and crevices. "We'll get you for this!" they cried to the One in authority. "We know who you are. We have friends in high places." But when he looked toward them, they drew the paving stones over their heads and were silent.

"You are whole," he said to the healed man. "Go in peace."

California Dreaming

I awaken from my midday sleep amongst the sunbathers lolling on the beach. Sun and sand conspire to keep me indolent and inert until the darkness falls. But something else draws me at least to test the water. After all, I needn't have come all this way just to sleep. So, reluctantly, I wrest myself out of the grasp of the beach, which by now has molded itself so comfortably to the shape of my body.

Surrounded as I am by such a cloud of somnambulant witnesses, shaking off the dirt and sand which cling so closely, I run with awkward step the path that is set before me, down to the water's edge—where I pause and reconsider. It is not too late to go back; no one has taken my spot yet. Sleep may still reclaim its own.

But I dab my big toe in the upper reaches of the last wave and think, "That's not too bad." So I prance around a bit in the retreating foam, along with the tiny tots. I chase a withdrawing wave, then flee in half-mock terror the next oncoming one. The little kids laugh at me.

Then I cut my toe on a rock or sharp shell, and sudden pain drives out the last vestiges of sleep. I hobble around in the ankle-deep water. The little kids laugh harder. Muttering under my breath, I notice other perils at my feet. So, I think, maybe if

I went a bit farther out, I'd get past the rocks. Or at least not be able to see them.

I resolutely stride out to meet the next wave, no longer turning to run at its approach, the ground squishing away between my toes. So long, sleepers and fainthearts.

As the crest moves toward me, I feel a mounting doubt about the wisdom of my current course, yet it is too late now to back away, so I brace myself. Still it throws me backwards, and, as the water rises to my chest, I realize for the first time how cold it is.

Now the wave is past and I stand waist-deep, shivering. Better go out a little deeper, where I can keep my shoulders under water and stay out of the air.

Less resolutely, more tentatively, I go further out, measuring the rise of the water on my body. I am past the breaking waves. Here they just lift me off my feet as they roll past. I hear them give a muffled crash behind me. My toes maintain a wary contact with the unseen bottom. Just so long as it's there, I feel reassured.

The bay stretches before me, the far shore lost to view behind the waves. I turn and look at the beach and notice how far away it looks, though I am only thirty yards offshore. Some older kids have a volleyball game going, and the lifeguard is bantering with the beach bunnies.

This is a good place to be. I will take a few strokes here, float a little bit, move parallel to the land. Yes, it is good here—no portable rock music, no one tripping over my toes as I try to sleep. I let my body go and untether my mind. Relaxing—letting the beneficent, colossal force of the water bear me up and move me along. I learn its rhythms, yield to its flowing. It soothes and strengthens me.

And now I will regain my toehold on the sandy bottom, reassuring myself of the old familiarities, that nothing has changed. Maybe it's time to head back to shore.

My foot descends to find its support, right there, right THERE, right where? My straining toe finds nothing. I've been fooled. I've drifted out of my depth. There is no bottom within reach. Panic possesses me as I thrash around for a foothold. Terror, anger, and self-hatred for having been lulled into such complacency, such trust. The more I struggle and fight, the more I sink under the surface.

The water's rhythms are unchanged, its motions timeless, ignoring my feeble efforts to contradict them. Threatening—the inexorable force of the water's weight bearing down upon me, crushing me into insignificance.

And if I continue to struggle, to rebel, to go down in a burst of glory and spite, then—how ironic—eventually the currents will deposit my body back on the beach, as inert and unconscious as the other sleepers, one of them, never to rise.

But I am no hero. I cry out for help, to no human lifeguard. I give up the fight and the pretense of coping, the sham of adequacy—as if a flea can do battle with an elephant, or a man with the sea. Shamelessly, I repeat the cry of a fellow water-treader: "Lord, save me!" No hand reaches down through the curtain of waters to haul me up beside him, but I am aware of a presence here with me below the surface, seeking my surrender. I resist—I argue that we can resolve that matter later when I can breathe again. Yet I continue to sink, and so, more in desperation than hope, I yield.

As I resign myself to destruction and meaningless dissolution in the depths, I find I have ceased thrashing and striving. I have stopped flailing in rage at my enemy as it snuffs out my life. The water again acts benignly on my body and I begin to rise. Resignation gives way to faith: he is not against me! Slowly the water bears me up to the surface. Faith gives way to hope: I may not die after all! And then my head breaks through and I see the sky—oh, sky, how long I have missed you, a gorgeous blue such as I never noticed before! With new eyes I gaze on it, and with new lungs breathe in the clear air.

I float there, at the mercy of the current, not fearful now. Resting, recovering, embracing that new presence. Then doubt intervenes; I am still out of my depth—what if I get a sudden cramp? Perhaps I'd better go closer to the shore.

But that which brought me up out of the darkness urges me out further still. And so I turn my feet toward land and take slow strokes away from the now-distant shore. The suddenly watchful lifeguard on his perch yells a warning through his megaphone. "You're in deep water out there!" But I go on.

A few voices from the crowd on the beach reach me. "Hey, come back! You fool, where do you think you're going?" But I heed them not, and strike out determinedly for the farther shore, for mine is a deep-water God.

Six Flags Over Jerusalem

And Jesus left that place and went up to Jerusalem, teaching and preaching about the Kingdom of God as he went. He joined the large crowds that were converging on the city for the holiday. Some of the throng followed him, hoping to see him perform the definitive Sign that would both establish his identity and bring God's Kingdom among them. Their spirits were high, the mood was festive, and gossip flowed freely. Their speculations were fueled by the silence of Jesus and the confusion of his disciples as to what would happen next. There was among the people the sense of being part of an irresistible movement that would wrest the land from the dual domination of foreigner and sin.

In their midst, the focus of their varied expectations, walked Jesus, the People's Prophet, at once accessible and inscrutable. The more he taught, the less they understood, but it didn't matter. Whatever he said, whatever he did, God was in it.

"James, tell us what's up. What's he going to do next?"

"Don't keep asking me. I don't have any idea."

"Oh come off it, man, you've been with him three years. Something big's going to happen, I know it."

"Good, then you tell me about it."

"Stop pretending. We're on your side. You can level with us."

"I keep telling you, Elias. None of us has a clue what he's going to do there."

"I'll bet he's going to call down an angelic army and drive the Romans into the sea."

"No, no!" interrupted another voice. "Jesus will proclaim himself king and lead the people into war."

James shook his head in exasperation. "You guys don't understand at all. He's very unpredictable. That's the one thing I've learned. Take any given situation—a simple meal, running into a leper or harlot on the road, getting stuck in a boat in the middle of a storm. You think, 'Any reasonable fellow will say such and such and do this and that.' And you stand there and watch him, and it doesn't come out that way at all."

Matthew cut in. "James is right. And even when the Master tells you something directly, it usually doesn't make sense. Then it happens just like he said, and you think, 'Oh, that's what he meant,' and wonder why you were too dumb to see it."

James agreed. "Yes, so there's no point trying to figure out what he'll do in Jerusalem, 'cause you're wasting your time. All you can be sure about is to expect the unexpected."

His listeners weren't satisfied. "Well, tell him to be careful, and also that we're with him."

"That's right, when he gives the word, we'll be ready."

"It's not going to be that way, I just told you!"

"Well, you tell him anyway. There's strength in numbers, and he can count on us."

James made his way up to Jesus. "These people make me so frustrated," he muttered. Jesus had been deep in his own thoughts, but now looked up at him and smiled. "What did you say, James?"

"Oh, nothing, Lord. It's just all the people with their crazy ideas and incessant demands."

Jesus laughed and put his arm on his shoulder. "Welcome, James! How often have I prayed the same words, and all the Father says is 'Patience.'"

"I feel caught between two worlds, Lord, and neither one makes sense to the other. What the people believe is lies and foolishness. I know that, but it's obvious and easy to follow. What you teach is true and lasting, but it's awfully hard to grasp and live out. Will I ever really understand?"

Jesus nodded. "Yes, James, you will, because you want to, and because I've invited you to."

There was a stir among the crowd as it drew near the city. The people looked up and saw the towers of the vast Temple complex rising above the rest of Jerusalem. Flags and banners fluttered from five of the highest points. The Temple was the heart of the city, of the nation, of the people. Not only was it the center of their religion, but the highest achievement of their civilization. Its physical monumentality symbolized its spiritual authority. And they all knew that somewhere deep inside those massive buildings, walled off from the view of sinful man, God Himself lived. The God of all the universe had taken up residence in a small room in the Temple, a place that none of them had ever set eyes on and never would. But by coming to His city and worshiping in His Temple, they could at least touch the outer fringes of His holiness.

Fathers pointed out to their sons the Temple buildings, mothers held up infants in their arms—even as their parents had done for them years ago. "This is it. Here we are. This is what it means to be a son of Israel."

That evening, Jesus and those with him camped within sight of the city walls. Jesus left his disciples and went off alone to sit under a tree. There he prayed, facing the city, the dying sun's rays bouncing off the buildings and towers. The disciples were in a somber mood, disturbed by the contrast between Jesus' solemn determination and the jocularity of the crowds. Around them, scattered over the hills, they could see the campfires of other travelers, and occasionally the noise of laughter or argument came to their ears. But they were nervous, impatient, fearful. They were accustomed to Jesus going off by himself at night to pray, but there was something different about him this time. A heaviness of spirit lay upon him. They sensed it without understanding it. No one wanted to talk or speculate about what tomorrow might hold, so they lay on their sleeping mats, each lost in his own fears.

At length, John got up quietly and went off to find Jesus. It was unheard of to interrupt Jesus in his solitude, so those who saw him get up thought he was merely going to relieve himself. But John walked quietly, timidly, away from the camp into the deepening darkness in the direction Jesus had gone. Soon he came out on a ridge over an open slope. Several large trees grew along the ridge, and, as he looked to either side, he saw beneath one of them the silhouette of a man sitting, his head bowed on his chest. John sat down where he was. Above him, the stars glinted their ancient, indecipherable message. Behind him, campfires and companionship solaced weary travelers. But here, silence, darkness, a place set apart. He waited.

"John." The silhouette spoke his name softly, questioningly.

"I'm sorry, Master." John stumbled out his apology. "I just wanted to be with you, to ask if there is anything I can do for you, or any of us can do. We feel so helpless."

There was a short pause, then Jesus said, "Come, sit with me." John got up, walked over, and sat beside him. Neither spoke. The peace of deep night descended. Presently John became aware of a sadness opening in his soul, an oppression beyond words.

Jesus spoke: "John, there is something you can do for me."

"Yes, Lord."

"Very soon now, the Son of Man will be handed over to the tormentor. Men will laugh and jeer. Women will curse him. Other men will run away and hide, some will stand afar off and look on in fear, and a few women will watch and weep for me. In that hour, John, will you stand close to me?"

"I will, Lord."

"It will comfort me to see your tears, John."

After a while John rose to rejoin the other disciples. As he stood up, the burden left him. He said nothing to anyone about what Jesus had told him.

The next day was the final one of their journey from Galilee. Jesus and those with him walked the last few miles up to the walls, then passed into the city. They joined thousands of other pilgrims from throughout Israel and the Empire. The streets were crowded and noisy, a hubbub of those seeking food and lodging, and of those selling wares or begging.

Jesus led his group toward the Temple complex, which was enclosed by a high wall. He stopped in the plaza in front of the main gate. A large sign had been erected there, with an arrow pointing to the gate. In several languages it proclaimed, *"This way to God."* Below it, a large crowd milled around. Several black-robed men sat in small booths with turnstiles in front of them. Hundreds of people were lined up to buy tickets from them for admission to the Temple area. Beggars, thieves, and fruit and candy vendors worked the lines of waiting worshipers. Still other people were massed up against the wall away from the entrance. These people were too poor to buy tickets or too unclean to be allowed inside. They had to be content with saying their prayers while touching the outside wall. However, no one considered this a guarantee of salvation.

Beyond this wall rose a fantastic assemblage of buildings, turrets, spires, galleries, and catwalks, all linked together to form an intricate but confusing network. From below, one could look up and see groups of people walking, running, or climbing on these various structures.

Jesus passed by the God sign and paused, surveying the mayhem of street vendors, tourists, beggars, Temple guards, ticket scalpers, and would-be worshipers. James took his hanging back as doubt and offered, "Lord, shall I get in line to buy some tickets? If you go in today, it's only three shekels a head, but if you wait 'til the Sabbath, the price goes up to five."

Jesus pursed his lips and appeared to consider the matter seriously. "No thank you, James. I think not. Let's just wait here a while." And he sat down on a wall under the sign and began to eat an orange.

There was a noticeable letdown among the people following him. They had come for miracles, healings, deliverances, and the unleashing of God's judgment. Jesus just sat there, eating a piece of fruit. So they sighed, put down their bags, spread out blankets on the ground, and prepared to rest.

"You know," Jesus said suddenly, thoughtfully, and his friends perked up. "The Kingdom of Heaven is like an orange."

"Oh, God," muttered Judas to Peter, "not more of these country fables. This is the city, this is big time, these are sophisticated people. This stuff isn't going to go over well at all."

"Hush up and listen," replied Peter.

"Many sections," Jesus was saying, "many seeds, one covering. First you must remove the skin, next you eat and are satisfied, and then you spit out the pips." He wiped his hands on a cloth.

"That was it?" whispered Thomas, on the other side of Peter. "What did he mean by that?"

"How do I know?" shrugged Peter.

"Well, ask him."

"You ask him."

"Not me, you know him better."

"That's exactly what I mean," interjected Judas. "He's rambling. This is not your friendly local synagogue—these men are doctors of the Law. They'll make mincemeat of this stuff."

Then Jesus stood up underneath the sign and in a loud voice began to teach the people. He told them stories of life and the Kingdom, and explained God's ways in simple language. A large crowd gathered around, drawn away from the tumult outside the gate.

After a while, Thomas nudged Judas and they turned to look behind them. Several black-garbed figures stood on the Temple wall watching them.

"We've been noticed," Thomas said with a frown.

"Yes," said Judas, "and I don't like the looks of this. Jesus has violated protocol by not even acknowledging those men of authority. Does he expect to win them over by teaching these dogs?"

"Well, we just have to trust he knows what he's doing, I guess."

"Sure, and if he doesn't and he's in over his head—what happens to us?"

Soon, several of the officials and other men of rank came over to listen. The people made way for them, but Jesus paid them no heed. Suddenly, one lifted his hand to get Jesus' attention.

"Rabbi, we know that you are a teacher and a man of exceptional gifts, yet your followers are sinners, common people, and those ignorant of the Law. If you were truly from God, you would have nothing to do with these people."

There were some angry murmurings from the crowd, but Jesus calmly replied, "Well now, you claim to be a teacher of the Law. Who do you think you are supposed to teach—angels?" The people laughed in derision. "These were the people you were appointed to lead, but you have preyed upon them instead. Therefore, I have come to gather my sheep and to judge the shepherds."

A great cheer went up from the crowd. The priest turned abruptly and walked away.

"This is not the way, not at all." Judas shook his head. "You just don't treat these people like that."

Thomas agreed. "I don't know what he's up to, either. You'd think these would be the last people he'd want to offend."

In the afternoon, Jesus stopped teaching and began healing some of the poor. A blind beggar received his sight, a lame woman could walk again, an insane man was cured; all to the great delight of the people.

"So what do you guys think of that?" asked Peter aggressively.

Judas nodded, impressed. "I'll say one thing about him—he's got power. And I've always known he had it. The question is, Does he know how to use it? Why waste it on cripples, when he could heal Herod of syphilis?"

Peter exploded, "Heal Herod? Why not let him rot?"

"True, I agree," said Judas. "He's a loathsome worm. But consider the political consequences. With Herod's favor, there'd be no stopping us. My point is, he's got to use his gifts for maximum impact and not squander them currying favor with the rabble. He can't go on talking back to the priests—sooner or later they'll nail him."

"Well, I don't know," Peter sighed, frustrated. "As far as I'm concerned, the less we have to do with those stuck-up prigs, the better. I've never been one for keeping all their laws anyway. They confuse me. I had better things to do, like catching fish."

Judas shook his head in disgust. "Fishermen! Jesus could have chosen scholars, fighters, thinkers—instead he picked peasants. That was his first dumb mistake." He walked off sulkily.

There was a sudden movement in the crowds, like the parting of a school of fish as a shark swims through it. James nudged Thomas. "It's the Man himself!" The disciples moved back and to the sides, clustering behind Jesus, who seemed totally unaware of the approach of the high priest's retinue. He was intent on touching a small child with a fever.

The high priest interrupted him. "You do not come to me, Jesus, so I have come to you."

Jesus looked up at him, but said nothing.

"So this is the famous prophet of Galilee." The priest made an effort to smile. "Welcome to Jerusalem, teacher."

"Do you indeed welcome me?" asked Jesus.

"Ah, that depends on you, my friend. If you come in peace, we welcome you. If you come to bring us trouble—well, we'll not speak of that. We have many things to talk about, you and I. There are questions and serious concerns that we have about you, and perhaps opportunities to help each other. But this is not the place for that. Please, will you be my guest and come with me into the Temple? No doubt it has been a while since you were last here. And I can get you into places you've never seen before. So please, come as my guest, and we can talk later."

"Very well," said Jesus, "I will come, but what about my friends here?"

"They can tour the Temple area as we talk in private." Turning to an assistant, he commanded, "Free passes for all the Galileans."

Then he turned and ushered Jesus through the crowd to the turnstiles. Guards and ticket-takers stepped aside respectfully as the large party passed into the outer courts of the Temple. Jesus had been here before many times, but each year there was something new. He paused to look up and around, but the high priest urged him on. "Come, we will go to my office in the central tower. From there you can see the whole place." Leaving behind the other priests and the disciples, he led Jesus into a large stone building. They went up five flights of stairs, which put them at a landing, above which rose a tower.

"Up and further up," the priest said, leading the way along a stone staircase spiraling up the inner wall. As he climbed, he nodded at Jesus. "You are a remarkable man," he said seriously. "Some of my advisors say you are a prophet, even the Messiah, blessed be his name, while others call you the devil. And now I have to decide who is right."

At last they came up into a spacious apartment with an outside porch capping the tower. The Temple flag fluttered from a pole on the porch. A servant brought wine and fruit. Jesus went to the porch wall and gazed around him. He could see for miles in each direction, far beyond the city walls. Right below was a jostling crowd of people, but here, though he could hear the noise plainly, he was abstracted from the clamor, transfigured into a spectator of his people's restless pilgrimage. He watched them surging this way and that, herded by Temple guides into large groups. From the ground it had looked confusing, but from above they looked like mice in a well-designed maze.

One group of men had followed a long passage between buildings and over walls and finally gained admittance to a courtyard where they presented their offerings and sacrifices. They then left by a side exit and were replaced by others. They were not really very close to the Temple itself, but that was as near as they could get by that route.

Another group had trekked nearly the whole circumference of the complex to another small courtyard, where they too presented their gifts. They then followed a parallel passage all the way back—in effect going twice around the area without ever getting near the center.

A large number of women was being ushered into a large building by the front gate. Once they had worshiped, they would have to wait out front until their husbands joined them. Women were not allowed to go into the inner courtyards.

Jesus watched a group of eager young men following yet another course—this one up and over walls and buildings, scaling them by means of ladders and steps, walking over roofs and along rope catwalks. They would eventually get to the wall of the Temple itself, if they managed to go the whole route.

The high priest spoke up. "It's quite impressive, isn't it?"

Jesus shrugged. "I find it rather confusing."

"Yes, it seems so at first, but there's a system to it. What seems random and chaotic is actually carefully planned out. Look—follow the people as they come through the gate. Immediately they are greeted by Temple officials who route them to the course proper to them: women over there, Gentiles to that round-about course that goes nowhere, cripples to the obstacle run—that was a challenge to design—tradesmen and farmers shunted there. Men of substance and rank go the central way, and a few we let into the Temple itself. Levites and rabbis also have their own access. The young and zealous we send up and down walls, and so forth. Something for everyone.

"The purpose is to give each person a satisfying sense of worship, a combination of aesthetics and devotional exercise, so that each goes away feeling he has come close to God, yet unsatisfied enough so that he'll return during the next festival and try it again."

"But how many ever make it into the Temple itself?"

"Oh, very few indeed, that's the whole point. We cannot have the feet of shoemakers and fishermen—oh, well, no offense, but you understand what I mean—we can't have just anybody setting foot in the Temple, getting close to the holiness of God. Our real duty here is not so much to assist people in their worship as to protect Him from them, to prevent them from getting too close to Him in their sin. Therefore, admittance to the Temple is restricted to those who have shown through diligent practice and elaborate self-purification that they will not contaminate His Presence."

Jesus frowned.

"Ah wait," the priest interrupted. "I know what you're thinking, that we short-change the common man. We are well aware of that. You see, we walk a very narrow line. On the one hand, we want to encourage the people to come here, to observe the laws as well as they can, to make the sacrifices and observe the customs. On the other hand, we recognize that their very presence is a danger to the holiness they have come to find here, because they themselves aren't holy. They would destroy the sanctity of the Temple if they were to set foot in it.

"That is why we have very carefully and ingeniously designed a religious experience for each type of person who comes, granting him just the amount of access to God that he is qualified for, and providing in return a sense of religious fulfillment and satisfaction. They come, they pay the admission fee, they walk or climb or run around a while until they get tired, they pay for a sacrifice, say a prayer, buy a silver or copper remembrance, and leave—happy that they have been here."

"And you think this kind of circus atmosphere is the way to worship God?"

"Please," the priest said, looking hurt, "not circus. We are very proud of what we've built here, and it has a most serious purpose. Worship is extremely important, we make sure of that and protect it. The common person—what does he know of worship? Most of the pilgrims visit the pothouses on their way to the Temple, and the whorehouses after they leave. So we make sure that all the unqualified are kept as far away as necessary so as not to interfere with those who are undefiled."

Jesus watched a lame man following a zigzag path that included fences to climb and water-filled trenches to jump across. It wound up and over and around, and ended back at the front gate. The high priest followed his gaze. "We call that Cripple's Run—all deformed people are kept well away from the Temple itself."

Jesus changed the subject abruptly. "You said you had questions to ask me."

"Ah, yes." The high priest grew pensive. "Questions, and perhaps opportunities. Actually, Jesus, I know quite a bit more about you than you might expect. I've been following your career for quite some time now. That's part of my job, keeping a finger on the religious pulse of the nation. So, naturally, when you began stirring up the popular enthusiasm, I had my agents check up on you. But their reports don't do you justice—I expected a demagogue, a rabble-rouser, or perhaps a firebrand like the

Baptist. But you're not like that, not what I pictured you to be. You have about you, how shall I put it? An air of wisdom, of seriousness of purpose. Now, I have been candid with you, so level with me. What are your real objectives? You've gained the nation's attention. What do you plan to do with it?"

"That is simple. I have come to do my Father's will."

The priest looked perplexed. "Your father? Joseph, the deceased carpenter?"

"No," Jesus shook his head. "Him, over there." He nodded toward the main Temple building.

The high priest grimaced. "Jesus, please. My friends tell me you are a gifted storyteller, that you can keep the people spellbound for hours. But please, speak plainly with me; what is your understanding of your mission?"

"I have come to restore the lost house of Israel."

"Yes, yes, but how? What are you going to do?"

Jesus smiled. "Watch and see."

The high priest shook his head in exasperation. "What I need to know is this: are you going to give me a lot of trouble, getting the people stirred up against the government, telling them God is about to drop heaven in their laps?"

Jesus gave him a quizzical look.

"It's so hard to tell from the reports of your teachings. Some of what you say is simple and ingenuous, for the people. I like it; it's on their level. Some of it is subtle and curious, showing you to be an innovator. But some of what I hear is radical nonsense. 'Take up your cross daily,' for instance. What cross? And what has a cross to do with knowing God? Or that bit about the Kingdom of God being here and now. That just incites the public against decency and order, not to mention responsible observance of the religious laws. Do you see my point? Piety is admirable, we need more of it. But fanaticism is dangerous. And I don't know where you stand."

Jesus was gazing out over the Temple grounds. "Where do I stand?" he asked, repeating the priest's question. "Right there—that's where I am," he said, pointing to the lame man who was now clambering over a wall. "Yes, I think I'd like to have a go at Cripple's Run before I leave."

The high priest sighed and said nothing. The two men looked at each other.

"Let me ask you a question," said Jesus.

"Shoot."

"You carry the weight of the nation on your shoulders."

"Yes," he said heavily.

"Not only the maintenance of temporal peace," Jesus said, "but, more importantly, the spiritual life of the country."

"Indeed."

"Would you like to have these burdens lifted from you?"

"Certainly I would, if it were possible. I would welcome your suggestions."

"Very well," answered Jesus. "Instead of you worrying about the Romans, the future of the nation, and the proper worship of the people, let me do it. Give your responsibilities over to me."

The high priest laughed out loud. "Yes, that would be a fine thing indeed, putting you as high priest in my place. What would the Sanhedrin think of that?" Then he realized Jesus wasn't joking and quickly caught himself. "Oh, it's not that I doubt your abilities, I assure you. In fact, I wish life were so simple. But of course that's impossible, unrealistic. I am an admirer of yours, but not a follower."

There was a pause. "However," the priest continued, "there may be a way we can work together. Let me make you an offer in return. It is the opportunity I spoke of when we first met. Jesus, I will be the first to admit that you have something we lack here. All this"— he gestured to the Temple complex — "is grand, wonderful, awe-inspiring, reverential, and so forth. But it lacks warmth, character, mystery, a heart. You have this quality—for lack of a better word, I'll call it rapport, a communicated enthusiasm for God that attracts people. We need you; we need this quality among us. But by the same token you need us—you need the security and backing, the approval and guidance we can provide. This is the seat of wisdom and learning and piety of our whole nation. Your spirit can enliven us while our heritage brings to you a maturity you could never achieve on your own. Look, it's the difference between being down there, milling around in the crowd and getting people excited for a season, and being up here, with an overall perspective, and with the power to influence a whole nation. I won't hide the fact you'd lose something by joining us—your independence, your ragtag bunch of followers—but you'd gain far more: the eyes and ears of the elders of Israel, not to mention the whole civilized world, would be open to you. In this way, you would be in a position to fulfill your ministry as never before—as you put it, to restore the lost house of Israel."

The priest waited for some sign of enthusiasm, some response from Jesus. But Jesus didn't look at him. He seemed lost in thought, his eyes wandering over the crowds below. The priest called a servant, who brought up a parchment. He unrolled it and beckoned Jesus to the other side of the porch. He spoke excitedly.

"Come, I've been doing some planning, daydreaming really. See that open patch of ground beside the money changers' quarters? Look what I'm planning to build there, as a part of our expansion plans. See the amphitheater, the seating for large crowds, the focus on the platform up front? I call it the Signs and Wonders Pavilion, Jesus, a place where the man on the street can come and touch the living mystery of our faith. A place for teaching, healing, parables, miracles—your whole ball of wax. But no longer disorganized and uncontrolled, but rather structured, deepened, incorporated into the Temple ritual.

"We will reroute the various runs to converge on the Pavilion, so that after each group of worshipers has run its course and made its sacrifices, we will funnel them into the seats, to receive teaching or healing or whatever—that personal touch. You understand. Think of it, Jesus. You've seen crowds before, but nothing like this: proselytes from Antioch and Athens, merchants returning from Rome, scholars from Alexandria, plus a continuous audience of the mightiest men of our nation—the Sanhedrin itself. And all of them, Jesus, all of them focused on the man who stands, under priestly approval and authority, on that stage. All of them focused on you, Jesus."

Jesus said nothing, but looked at the parchment drawing. Marble columns, a central stage, rising tiers of seats as in Greek and Roman stadia, and from the top of the structure, a flagpole rose, from which a pen-and-ink flag fluttered—the sixth flag above the Temple complex.

The priest was still waiting expectantly for some response, even a flicker of interest. Jesus rolled up the parchment and put it aside.

"Signs and wonders. You want miracles. But the only sign I shall give you is that of the prophet Jonah."

"Jonah? What sign did he do?" asked the priest, dismayed and perplexed.

"You cannot build anew on an old foundation. You cannot build the Kingdom of God on the works of man. But if you will destroy this temple, I will raise it up again in three days."

The priest gazed at him, stupefied. "What, destroy the Temple?"

"You cannot mix new wine with old. I have brought you the new, but to drink of it you must first pour out the old."

The priest could barely control his rage. "So now I know," he said. "You are mad; you're crazier than my advisors warned me. Get out of this holy place, or by . . ." He swallowed his anger. "I'll have you thrown off this tower."

Jesus turned and walked alone down the stone stairs into the Temple area, past guards, through long halls, to the outer concourse where crowds were being routed past the stalls of the money changers and souvenir vendors. A few of the disciples saw him leaving and ran to catch up with him.

"Master, we've been around the grounds twice. Matthew even got to touch the Temple wall."

But they saw by his stern face and rapid steps that something was wrong.

"What did the high priest say, Lord?" John asked.

Jesus looked sadly at John. "He said No, John." Then he kept walking, through the gate, past the turnstiles, and down the street.

***

It was the next day, early in the morning, that he returned. The weather was good, the Passover feast was underway, and Temple officials were expecting record crowds. The street vendors had laid in double supplies in preparation for the throngs of pilgrims.

Historians and literary critics alike have long debated the significance and appropriateness of the incident, but there is no disputing the fact that on that morning, from somewhere, Jesus obtained a Caterpillar bulldozer. As he drove it rumbling through the streets, the astonished and terrified crowds fled before him. This was no mad rampage, however. Jesus carefully maneuvered the heavy machine through the streets until he got to the large sign pointing directly to the Temple. And there he paused a moment, turned the bulldozer in the exact direction the sign indicated, raised the massive blade, and put the machine in gear. Down the broad main concourse he came, a slow and invincible advance.

People melted away to either side.

"Stop!" yelled a ticket-seller. "You'll hit the gate."

Smash! The blade ripped out the bars and turnstiles, then the very gate itself fell. The bulldozer churned into the outer court of the Temple. Before it lay the maze of different runs. Jesus neither paused, nor turned to the right or left. He barreled through everything that lay before him, breaking into the women's section and out the other side, bashing down the wall that segregated foreigners. Towers and catwalks fell as their support pillars were knocked out. The central section of Cripple's Run was plowed under.

Scores of guards and officials rushed to the scene, shouting and shaking their fists in anger, throwing rubble after him—but no one dared to get in front of the bulldozer. He came to the street of the money changers, animal sellers, and trinket vendors. As the steel treads crushed the wood and fabric stalls, outraged merchants joined the mob of priests and officials chasing him. But no one could stop him.

At last he reached the main courtyard. Before him rose the Temple itself. Here Jesus paused. Behind him lay a straight path of destruction and chaos. The crowd closed in. Angry men shouted to kill the blasphemer. Jesus raised the blade and started the bulldozer up the marble steps. It ground into them, scarring and cracking them as it climbed. To the horror of the people, he smashed through the massive doors at the top. One guard beat frantically and helplessly at the bulldozer with his sword.

Another threw his spear at the driver and hit Jesus in the chest. But the machine was set in gear, and it continued to move forward, carrying with it the body of Jesus, breaking through the inner partitions of the Temple until it ripped apart the sacred curtain and stalled in the Holy of Holies itself.

And now at last there was silence. The destruction had ended, the engine's roar had quit. Temple officials wandered around in confusion and shock. Several elderly priests knelt in the dust, tearing their clothes and crying out to God. Frantic merchants tried to retrieve their spilled coins and lost animals. From the ruined Temple doors, one could stand and look down a perfect beeline of devastation, reaching all the way to the signpost.

And then they came, first just one or two, then a trickle, then an excited crowd. People who had been waiting in the plaza for the gates to open stepped cautiously through the breach once the dust had settled. First the adventurous, then the more timid started to surge through the gap. And they followed the tread marks, not the broken-down detours, even up the Temple steps.

An elderly woman spoke to the beggar beside her. "I've been here many times, but never this close."

He replied, "I never even got in the gates. They kept me out as unclean."

But it was a thief who had been working the crowds who first came out of the inner courts and up the broken stairs. Passing through the doors, he followed the path of the bulldozer right into the heart of the Temple. Others followed him, while the priests and guards stood helpless on the periphery.

"Caiaphas, should we not stop this vandalism?" asked one distraught captain.

"What's the point?" The high priest shrugged as he watched the increasing numbers of people pressing to get up the Temple steps. "The holiness is gone, the sanctity is forever destroyed. It is finished."

***

But it wasn't, quite. For three hundred years, people streamed freely through the breached walls, following the bulldozer tracks. Then suddenly, the noise of stone chisels and hammers.

"What is going on?" a young military officer was asked.

"Nothing much. Just a little clearing out of the rubble, beautifying the route. It's the Emperor's orders."

And a new order of priests rose up and erected a few fences and crowd-control barriers, a wall or two, and some detours. Then they decided that only they should have access to the Temple itself, so a large wall was built around the central building to keep the general public away. Even the turnstiles were re-installed. God lay re-entombed in his little room of gold and stone.

A thousand more years passed and all traces of the bulldozer's path were covered over. The courses were re-established, and six flags flew from the towers. But a monk appeared at the head of a column of troops who were trundling a battering ram, and they began a furious assault on the gates. They broke through and marched on the Temple itself, following the original route Jesus had created long before. Once again towers and barriers fell, and access to the Holiest Place was regained. There was great joy and celebration that the ancient way was recovered.

But the soldiers no sooner laid down their weapons than they picked up building tools. A little cleaning up, a little straightening and smoothing of rough places, the setting up of a wall against all who had fought against them. Guards were posted at checkpoints to turn away those who did not know the proper passwords. Year by year, stone by stone, the walls rose again.

Three hundred years passed, and a mighty storm came up and began to pound the barricades. The high wind toppled towers and steeples and broke down fences. Once again, those kept outside had free access to the Temple itself. But the very people who rushed in through the breaches at once set about rebuilding the courses to their own liking, a brick here, a wall there, and gates to limit access.

So it goes even to our own day. Great tumult and confusion, much noise and activity. Some are tearing down, some are building up. Huge towers are built, only to fall flat in a single generation. Broad and impressive courses are laid, only to be vacated and abandoned. The street of the money changers is as crowded as ever. And the people themselves rush to and fro, seeking an entry, looking for a way to get close to the center, trying one route and then another. As in Jesus' day, there is confusion, there is deception, there is frustration. But the sign still stands pointing the way, the bulldozer tread marks are still visible on the ground, the Temple curtain remains torn, and the Spirit yet strives to set free the holiness of God.

The Cruise

The loud blast of the ship's horn woke Catherine from her nap in a chair in the cabin on the main deck. Looking out the window, she could see they were entering port. A green-bordered shoreline had replaced the endless, empty horizon she'd stared at dismally only a few hours before.

David noticed she was awake and came over to her.

"How are you feeling, Mother?"

"All right," she replied weakly. This had been a rough trip for her. "I want to go outside."

"There's no hurry," Janice, David's wife, said quietly. "You can rest here until you feel better."

It was too much trouble to argue. Catherine started to get to her feet. Immediately, her family came to her aid, one on each side, David speaking in an overly encouraging voice that both amused and irritated her. It reminded her of her own tone toward him forty years before, when she had been teaching him to walk.

"Slowly, Mother, you're doing great. Let Janice carry your handbag. No? All right then, lean more on me. Here's the handrail. Let's take it slow, one step at a time."

He kept up his chatter until she was on deck, with both of them wrapping their arms protectively around her. They led her to the shoreward rail, where she was refreshed not only by the breeze and sun, but even more by the close prospect of land.

David hurried off to get a deck chair for her, which she ignored when he brought it. Janice slipped her own jacket around Catherine's shoulders. Though Catherine didn't need it, she enjoyed the touch of the younger woman, the sense of life and health in her encircling arm, in contrast to her own illness and waning strength. She wanted to tell Janice "Thank You," but didn't know how to convey the gratitude she felt for her presence and for her love for David. So she said nothing, but clasped Janice's hand and stared at the shore moving past.

The ship blew another long blast. Now the town was in view. Catherine could see a number of buildings with hills behind them, and roads up the hills, and mountains far beyond them all. She felt a great yearning to be there, to be ashore, to have solid ground under her again, instead of being stuck in this awful, topsy-turvy, up and down world where she could not even stand up without help.

David's voice came again. "Is this all right, Mother?"

She nodded.

"I think she's looking better already. Don't you think so, Janice?"

"The fresh air will do us all some good," agreed Janice. "That room was stuffy."

Now Catherine could see the pier toward which the ferry was heading. The town slowly took shape before her eyes. "It looks a bit like a Mediterranean fishing village," she thought to herself. She was relieved that it wasn't like the cluttered, jumbled city they had left behind.

The boat cut its engines. Other passengers and crew lined the rail as the ferry prepared to dock. But as they came nearer to the shore, she saw a large crowd waiting on the wharf.

"Oh dear," she thought, "how can I get through all those people?"

Her children noticed the sudden tension in her body and stepped closer.

"You're doing great, Mom," David said.

Catherine sighed. David's forced cheerfulness was annoying. They were closer to land now. The boat's engines reversed, and the water swirled under the stern. Some of the people on shore were pointing up at her and waving. She waved back feebly, then realized with a start that she knew some of them.

"How stupid of me," she said. "Of course Jack would be here."

"Mother, would you like to sit in this chair?" persisted David.

She ignored him and waved at her husband. Jack stood there beaming, not able to wave because of the large bouquet of flowers he was carrying. Good old Jack, she smiled—faithful, reliable, and kind. He looked healthy, far better than she herself felt.

Jack tilted his head to his left. She looked beside him and saw her sister Joellen. Joellen! Why of course she would come, and in the front row at that. There she stood, stolid, stern-faced, holding a gigantic fruit basket spilling over with apples, oranges, bananas, and grapes—enough to feed a boatload of monkeys. Poor Joellen, always absolutely determined to do the right thing, regardless of who or what stood in her way—and forgetting that Catherine could no longer eat most kinds of fruit.

She scanned the rest of the crowd, many of whom seemed to be looking at her. How distressing! Had the whole village turned out? She caught sight of her dear friend Margaret waving her kerchief.

"Hello, Margaret," she called cheerily.

Margaret was wearing a lovely new outfit, she noticed. "I wonder where she got it? I'll have to go shopping with her when I feel able," she thought. Then she realized that everyone in the crowd was dressed in their Sunday best. With embarrassment, she looked down at her own plain and soiled frock.

"This will never do; it's awful," she said disgustedly.

"Mother, what's wrong?" asked David anxiously.

"Nothing, nothing," she said, shaking her head impatiently.

Just then the boat bumped against the pilings. Ropes were thrown to men on shore and made fast. The crowd cheered louder and some threw bright streamers. A band that she hadn't noticed at the back of the throng struck up a loud marching tune.

"Oh, this is horrid!" she exclaimed. Truly, she did not have the energy to put up with this commotion.

"Janice, she's in pain. Help her!" said David urgently.

"I don't know what's wrong," Janice protested.

The gangplank rumbled out onto the dock. Catherine began to shuffle along the deck towards it. At once, her family came to support her on either side.

"We'll take her inside to lie down, and I'll call for the doctor," David said.

They would have carried her past the ramp and back to the cabin if she hadn't stopped and grasped the arm of the deck steward who stood at the head of the gangway.

"Let me help you down the ramp," he said. "It's very uneven."

He placed his arm around her shoulder, gently but firmly removing David's and Janice's hands.

"Mother!" cried Janice.

"Don't go!" cried David desperately.

Frantically they reached after her to pull her back, but she had already started down the incline beside the steward. Another loud cheer went up from the people on shore. She looked around—wasn't anyone else disembarking?

Below her, the water swirled between the ship and the pier. She felt suspended over a great chasm. She grew frightened—what if she had another of her weak spells right now and fell off the narrow ramp? She tightened her grip on the steward's arm and looked back at the ship. David and Janice were hugging each other and sobbing. They looked so pitiful, she forgot her fear. She felt she needed to say something to cheer them up.

"I'll try to write," she called out, but they didn't seem to hear.

Turning around, she faced the pandemonium on shore: whistles, cheering, streamers, oompah! oompah! whomp! whomp! Really, it was dreadful!

She continued reluctantly down the ramp, one hand on the rail, one on the arm of her escort. The steward stepped ashore first and turned to help her. She looked up at him to express her thanks, and saw his face beaming down at her. "Why, I know you!" she said in amazement. He laughed at her surprise. He had been there all the time on the boat with her and she hadn't recognized him. The faces of the crowd melted away in the warm welcome of his eyes and smile. Letting go of the railing, she reached unsteadily towards him, and he took both of her hands in the firm grasp of his own pierced ones.

Thru Hiker

She lingered in the open field, watching the wildflowers against a backdrop of trees, and above them the snow-capped mountains over which she had hiked. It was all a delight, a joy, a constant variation of beauty. There was no hurry, no pressure, no rush—she could stop as often as she wanted, to absorb more of the grandeur of each moment. When she had first set out on the trail, she had wandered and stumbled and tired so quickly. She had often failed really to see the land around her. To see with the eye alone is merely to note the outward form, but to see with the heart is to touch the inner life. The former is the sightseeing of a tourist, the latter the journey of a pilgrim. Sometime during the last few months, somewhere over the last several score miles, she had made the transition.

She shifted her backpack and looked back the way she had come. The slight trail was soon lost to sight in the hills and trees. Yes, she'd been each step of the way, even through those massive mountains. All on her own, too. The awareness of her achievement still amazed her. She was not the same person she had been on the other side of those cliffs, facing them indecisively, hoping somehow to skirt them rather than ascend them. But she had stayed on the path, she'd hung in there, sometimes not daring to look either back and down or forward and up. Yet she had conquered them; they were her servants now. And the fruits of that achievement were feelings of joy for whatever lay around her and of confidence to face whatever lay ahead.

She turned and looked ahead along the path, not in fear but in anticipation. She could see the reflection of water glimmering through the trees. What would it be? A creek, a lake, a river? Yes, it was a river, coming down like herself from those great mountains. Weeks ago she had soaked her feet in an icy mountain stream, and here once again she encountered it grown fresh and full. In the same way, she herself had been enriched and invigorated as she had followed the twisting course of her own path down from the heights. She would camp by the river tonight; it would be a pleasant reunion and communion of friends.

She began walking towards it. How she loved water in all its forms, to see its rushing vitality or quiet stillness, to feel its coldness against her sweaty feet. Well, except for the coldness of rain at night, when it soaked her tent and sleeping bag—that she could do without! She recalled passing a pristine mountain pool, perhaps never before seen by human eyes. It lay as a living thing in the heart of the mountains, and she had refrained from drinking from it or even touching its perfection.

She had walked beside puddles, streams, and rivers, crossing and recrossing some of them, never tiring of their conversation. And someday, she hoped, she would see the ocean itself—the vast, infinite gathering of all waters. Surely, if she followed this trail and the river far enough, it would lead her to the ocean. Maybe so, maybe not. But if it did, what then? Would the path dead-end in the sea, or would there be a way across? Having made it over the mountains, she no longer believed in dead ends.

In all these miles, in all these weeks, she had been alone, completely by herself. But this was not a trial to her. On the contrary, the solitude had answered a need in her soul to get away from people and their demands. This trek represented an escape, a departure from the familiar, from everything "back there" in the past. Once, all that had been her present. It was her whole existence; it was everything she knew about life—and now it had completely ceased to exist for her, a distant and harmless bad dream. Her life had really begun when she had taken that first step away from home.

Well, it was only going to be a stroll, a brief interlude from normal life, a bypath to a scenic overlook. How long, how many years, had she passed by that same turnoff and been too rushed to stop? Yet this time she had turned aside for just a moment, paused a few minutes to look at the view. She had stood there and seen a breathtaking vista of hills and valleys and trees stretched out before her. And there, leading down from where she stood, was a trail, faint and unmarked, maybe nothing more than a deer trail, leading out into the valley before her. It beckoned to her with a personal invitation to come and walk upon it. And she knew, as she stood there, that she would return and do so.

Weeks later she had come back to that spot, wondering if the trail was still there, prepared for a short hike. She spent an hour walking along it before returning to the trailhead. Her feet had hurt and she was out of breath, but there was also a sense of hope and excitement that she had been missing for a long time. An adventure was awaiting her. She came back frequently and hiked longer stretches, passing the valley, going through a forest and over a low ridge. From the ridge she could see a range of mountains in the distance. The trail led towards them, still unmarked and narrow, but distinct to her eyes. As she gazed at the far-off peaks, she knew she was going to climb them, just as the moment she'd first seen the trail she knew she was going to follow it.

Now she laughed at herself as she recalled those early days. What a tough old bird she'd become, hardened by days of climbing up the rising path, pulling herself up by rocks and roots, sleeping in crevices, drinking from waterfalls—finally, in triumph, gaining the heights. What an unparalleled exaltation of spirit that had been! Truly she had been reborn in that moment; there had been a casting off of her former self and a recognition of what had been building within her during the labors of the past weeks. She had even given herself a new name, a "trail handle"—Mountain Strider—and had said it only half-jokingly. Then she crossed those mountains and descended into the meadows.

"Tough old bird?" she asked herself. Not true—tough, yes, but there was nothing old about her, rather a recovered youthfulness and exuberance. During her journey, she was not being worn down, as if she were the weary veteran of a long march, but she was being strengthened. Every step, every day, built something into her, and took something away—that old life, the old doubts and fears, the indecisiveness, dreariness, and purposelessness.

This was part of the fruit of her loneliness. Sometimes far away she had seen roads or villages and people moving in them, but she had kept to herself, coming into a town only to buy supplies. Once she had passed a mountain cabin alongside her trail—"her" trail? She felt a rightful sense of proprietorship about it now; it belonged to all who walked it. There was a man her own age standing in front of the cabin. He had been chopping wood but paused to watch her pass. His beard and long hair and old plain clothing showed him to be a long-time resident, probably another escapee like herself. She nodded to him, but said nothing and walked on, respecting the silence he had found for himself.

And she herself—how she treasured this most holy quiet, the cessation of human noise. For once the voices had ceased, the bustle and clamor and pettiness, then the silence had begun to speak to her. It was the wind that spoke, but not alone, for it used many tongues—the leaves on the trees, the boughs and trunks, the grass and flowers that it moved across. It was the river that spoke, itself a master of a thousand languages, from obscure dialects in small eddies to the common tongues of great rapids.

Now she set up camp by the river among the trees, so as to be sheltered from the night chill. She had her fire going and her kettle out, then her frying pan. She would cook pancakes, she decided, and eat them as the sun set beyond the trees on the far side of the river.

In the evening, a light mist settled over the low areas near the river. But that was all right, she assured herself. It wasn't like the other stuff, her one enemy on this adventure, that awful dense fog that frightened her and caused her to lose all sense of the trail and her surroundings. When it descended on her, she would stop in her tracks, sit down, bury her head in her arms and pray for it to go away. Sometimes it hung around for several hours, accompanied by a damp chill, but eventually it always lifted. She would anxiously seek out the trail ahead of her, as if it might have disappeared forever in the darkness. But always it was still there, and she was able to continue her hike. Occurrences of this fog had been most frequent during the first weeks of her journey, and most terrifying when she was crossing the mountains.

Otherwise she had found nothing to fear, which was surprising, since she had never considered herself an outdoor person. No animals had bothered her. Even the mountain itself had been more fearful in prospect than in actuality. It had been hard work to climb, steep at times, and she had often been to the edges of high cliffs, but she had never had a sense of great danger as long as she stayed on the trail.

She went to sleep in the shadow of a couple of large elm trees, the river hushing itself at her feet. Shortly before dawn, she woke with a familiar sense of foreboding. Cold air penetrated her tent. It was more than the night mist. She was surrounded by an impenetrable curtain of silent gray. Fear gripped her as she came fully awake.

***

Two women were bending over her and lifting her up. "Bath time, Rose. Ready, Pauline?"

"Yes."

"One, two, up!"

The nurses lifted her out of bed into a wheelchair, then pushed it through a door and down the hall to a small room with a tile floor and bath. They removed her gown, and Pauline turned on a sprayer. Rose caught sight of her reflection in a mirror on the door—a limp, gaunt body, a tangle of white uncombed hair, and wide, helpless eyes.

***

"It's hard to say, Mrs. Emerson. Physically she's weak, but holding her own. I really can't give you a definite prognosis—maybe weeks, maybe a few months. It's unlikely, but possible."

"But she doesn't even recognize me or the children."

"That's true, and she will not improve. Because of the progressive nature of the disease, her periods of awareness will be fewer."

"She just sits there, with no life in her, no spirit, her eyes looking out the window. After our last visit, my son called her a vegetable. Is she even a person anymore?"

The doctor sighed. "I hope so. I think it matters that you care, and that you come. As far as any hope for improvement, I'm sorry to say that I cannot give you any."

The woman left the office and walked down the hall, where Rose was being returned to her room. She was wheeled to the patio door where she could look outside.

The fog was lifting now, the light was shining, and she could once again see the river.

"Good-bye, Mother. We'll come again in two weeks, when Robert gets home from college."

She bent and kissed Rose on the cheek and brushed the hair back from her face.

"I love you, Mom."

Then she got up quietly and left the room. Rose didn't see her go; she was looking out the patio door into the garden beyond, at the flower bushes and small fountain, and at the path that led between them.

Jairus' Daughter

I lay there on my bed feeling ill. My mother sent for the physician, but he found nothing wrong. "Stop pretending," he said. "Get up, do your work." But I could not rise or even speak a word. I lay flat and looked at the ceiling.

They brought in my brothers and sisters, my friends. "Come on, get up, play with us, stop being lazy. Don't just lie there and do nothing." But they didn't understand that I was pressed flat on the bed, squashed under a mighty fist that held me there, pressing my chest, taking away my breath.

My father came in. "Daughter, Daughter, what is the matter? Why are you suffering?" I opened my mouth to speak and felt my life flowing away. Then came the rabbi and the elders of my synagogue. Their grim faces surrounded my bed, solemn as the angel of death. They muttered prayers and chanted. Oil was daubed on my forehead and palms. They grew silent, they waited. The darkness increased. They shook their heads and shuffled out.

And now I was sinking down into the depths of my bed, far down into the dark. The covers closed over me, my mother's anxious face receded from me. The weight on my chest was so great I could no longer take a breath.

Far, far over my head came the shrill and bitter noise of crying women, with loud sobs and wailing. But I was leaving them, traversing a rough and rocky path in a cliff wall, winding around and down. The fist on my chest had become a hand behind me, pushing me, urging me on faster. I found myself descending into a dark valley and saw a great crowd assembled below. Hands reached up to grasp me and show me to my place.

Just then the crying stopped, the wailing ceased. I stumbled over a rock in the trail, tried to regain my balance, but slipped and tumbled head over heels—landing on my bed! Where was the valley and the dark crowd of people, the grasping hands? Where was that fist pushing me down into the ground? There was light in my eyes and I found myself staring directly into the face of a man who stood over me. But his eyes—they were points of fire. He leaned over me and took my hand. As he did so, a gust of wind blew through my window, straight into my mouth and down into my chest, filling my lungs. "Little One," he said intently, those eyes not leaving mine, "Little One, rise up, your home is not with the shades but with the living." There was strength in my arms and legs to do as he said, and I got up, still transfixed by his face. He led me to the door and I saw in the outer room my family and friends. They had been standing around crying and talking about the funeral arrangements, but as we came out of the bedroom, they became utterly still. On their faces I saw shock, amazement, disbelief.

Before they could say anything, the man who held my hand said sternly, "Give her something to eat." A couple of the neighbor women started to rush into the kitchen, but he stopped them. "Do you love her?" he asked abruptly.

"But of course, Rabbi—she is our daughter," said my father.

"Then give her something to eat."

Again, several people started for the kitchen. "Sir, we've got plenty of food; she can have all she wants."

Again he stopped them and repeated the question. "Do you love her?"

My friends and neighbors spoke up. "Yes, of course, we love her dearly."

And he repeated, "Then give her something to eat." There was an embarrassed silence. No one moved.

And then my mother understood and said softly, "Yes, Rabbi, we love her," and she came up and embraced me to her heart.

Identity Theft

Young woman, a moment of your time please. No, we haven't met, but I've been watching you for quite some time now—how hard you work, your diligence and character, your honesty and intelligence. And I can say with the utmost respect that you are truly an exceptional person—yes, you are, now don't be modest—deserving of honor and recognition. Look at all your accomplishments here; it's not only that you achieve so much, but that you do each task so well. It amazes me that you manage to give full attention to even the humblest task, and thereby endow it with both nobility and beauty.

And thus I wish I could be the bearer of good tidings to you, to brighten your life as you have mine, but regrettably I cannot, for I am greatly disturbed as I have pondered your situation. Don't be alarmed—there is nothing wrong with you, not in the least. It is your circumstances in life, your surroundings, your role, that trouble me, not you yourself. I have no word of criticism at all to direct toward you, save this: how could such an excellent individual allow herself to become trapped in such a hopeless, dreary existence?

Please let me explain. It is not that you face terrible danger or desperate straits. If you did, it would be far easier for me to convince you of your peril. It is, rather, that you are in a position that isn't suited to you. You are confined in a role that isn't up to the measure of your abilities. They have put the right person in the wrong job. And you don't realize it, because slowly and inevitably they are draining out of you the very energy, intelligence, and creativity which would enable you to rise above your current dead-end position. So, eventually, you will be not only confined in, but defined by, their expectations of you, and at that point the game is over, there is no hope for you.

You are surprised at hearing this? Yes, no doubt you are. But I've seen many distressing things that seem to have escaped your attention, and that is why I've been bold to address you directly. All of this has been happening below the surface, beneath the level of your awareness—because they know that if you knew the truth you wouldn't put up with it any longer.

Can you realize the extent to which you have allowed others to run your life? You are eager in response to their demands, you willingly perform every function asked of you—and this is entirely commendable, but there needs to be as well a critical faculty in you. You cannot just go on taking whatever comes, whatever others dish out; you have got to develop the capability of evaluation conjoined with your aptitude for ready service. So that, when a request is made of you, you first think: (A) Is the request reasonable? (B) Is it feasible in the light of my other duties? (C) Is it something that I can do well, does it match my abilities? and (D) most important of all, Is it something I want to do, does it meet my needs in some way? That is how you become a participant in the process of life, rather than the mere functionary which you have been until now.

Right now, you are letting others ask these questions and make these decisions for you. You have been doing just what they think you are able to do and only what they want you to do, and they have given you in return only what they want to give. And you have spoken not a word in protest! Let us grant the fact that they care about you, that they have you do those tasks they think you do best, and that they provide you with all they think you need to live on. The point is, why don't you have a say in any of this? After all, who knows better than you what you need, or what you are capable of accomplishing? But you have been satisfied to take their assessment on all counts, never questioning their judgment! This baffles me—I find it both incomprehensible and tragic.

It is plain to the objective observer that you have been used, no, misused, even abused. Again, I am not talking about violence directed against you. What you cannot see taking place is both subtle and dangerous. Your real nature, your true self, is being denied, sacrificed, squandered, on behalf of these others, all with your own unconscious complicity. You have let them determine your self-worth!

Does this make even a little sense to you? I am trying to call forth in you a sense of your own uniqueness and identity, your own worth and power, apart from what you receive from others. *You* are valuable, *you* are powerful, *you* are worthy—*you* have special qualities and abilities just waiting to come forth and be expressed. Yet here you are, day after day, plodding along in benign, benighted servitude, wasting and denying your own gifts. It is a shame; it is a sin!

May I make a suggestion—nothing major, nothing upsetting to you—that will make a big difference in the long run? I want to suggest a change in attitude first. Keep on in your current course of life on the surface, but resolve to gain control of your thought life. Recognize yourself as an independent person, not a mere extension of others' wants. See yourself as distinct from them. Identify your own strengths, weaknesses, desires, and dreams. Don't merely reflect the ideas of others and their expectations of you. This is the seed of selfhood, so nurture it carefully and deliberately. Put down deep roots into your own being.

Then, after you have established some idea of self and identity, a sense of who you truly are as a person, you can move on to the next stage of actually releasing your hidden strengths. The seed now sends its shoot above the surface for the first time. The invisible self is made visible as you gain control of your own body. I am speaking not merely of your sexual subjugation, which in itself is deplorable, but more specifically of your work and the fruits of your labor. On the one hand, regarding sexuality, you have let them determine this most private aspect of your identity. How dare you allow those who are not female to define the place and work of a woman? It is for you, and you alone, to define your own nature; there is no precut design to follow. You must reveal to them what a woman is, in accordance with your desires, not theirs.

Now as regards your daily work, the labor and toil you do from sunup until sundown and even beyond—it is painfully obvious that you are once again being mistreated. You work hard and well, but look at the meager results. All the benefit and credit go to others, while you are given just enough sustenance to maintain yourself in healthy bondage. It is not just the quantity of work required of you. As I've tried to make clear, it is the nature of the tasks themselves, and the fact that you have no say in what you do. It is for you to choose the kind of work you want to do, and when or whether to work at all.

Wake up, Child. Come alive to the power of your own body!

This is what control of your body means: once you have identified your hopes and desires and developed a sense of self, you begin to alter your behavior to achieve those goals. You use your strengths to gain what is valuable to you. And no one else—myself included, of course—has the right to tell you what that is. You are the one who knows yourself best, and you must set your own course.

And this brings us to the final stage, the glorious outcome of the journey I am describing to you. Once you have achieved awareness of your own thoughts and control over your own body, you are ready and able to define your own destiny. This is the real objective, the ultimate good that you can but dimly see at this point. This is the result of the process of self-liberation, to be able to exercise the right of self-determination. You haven't given much thought to this, have you? Of course not. You never even knew the option existed, because they have kept this knowledge from you so that they can determine your future for you. But when you have grown enough in the way I've indicated to you, when you are strong enough to rule your own life, nothing can stand before you and your power of choice.

And this is what they are afraid of. This is why they keep you under a benevolent domination. They know that once you realize who you really are, you will become like them and they won't be able to take advantage of you any longer.

Well now, I ask your pardon, for I see that I have frightened you with all this talk of worth and power. You are not accustomed to thinking of yourself in these terms. That is because you are thinking their thoughts and not your own. I paint pictures of a glorious future and yet you remain chained to a tawdry reality. But self-realization is not as hard or as long a process as it sounds. As you move in the right direction, power will come to you that you had no idea you possessed.

The important thing right now is the matter of decision. Will you continue as you have in the past, or are you willing to start on the road to freedom? Of course, if you don't find that what I've said is true—although it is, because I've taken this journey myself—you can always return to the security of safe and familiar patterns. No one is asking you to sign your life away. The most reasonable thing, in my opinion, is to test what I've said to you, think it out for yourself, and make your own decision. I have confidence in you, in your intelligence and courage, that you will make the proper choice.

> So when the woman saw that the tree was good for food, and that it was a delight to the eyes, and that the tree was to be desired to make one wise, she took of its fruit and ate; and she also gave some to her husband, and he ate (Gen 3:6 RSV).

No God

It was in my eighth grade Political Doctrines class that the disturbance occurred. We were studying the great qualities of our Nation—her oppressed past, her blossoming present, her glorious future. In contrast were the lesser nations and subject peoples already conquered, and a few remaining countries still to be absorbed or obliterated. What contempt we had for them, for the decadence of their culture and the weakness of their will. What could they offer against the splendor of our Country and the wisdom of our Party?

"The lesser nations collapsed," our teacher explained, "because the people took what rightly belonged to the State and devoted it to myths, to a superstitious being called 'God.'"

This term was not familiar to most of us, so the teacher told us to look up the word in our dictionary.

"God: a concept held by primitive nations as a substitute for the People; a nonmaterial, invisible and nonexistent fairytale figure endowed with all the qualities of power and goodness that rightfully belong to the State."

This concept was hard to grasp, so the teacher explained it to us.

"Look, after we get up in the morning and before we go to bed at night, what do we do? We stand facing the picture of our Leader and dedicate ourselves to her service. The corrupt peoples used to devote themselves to this invisible being called God.

"Before we eat our meals, what do we do? We thank the Party for our food and promise to use our energy to serve it. The defeated peoples stupidly believed their food came from God, even though it was their own hands that grew it.

"When we lack understanding or need help in some way, we go to our section officer, who handles our request and gives us the official approval or denial. Our enemies foolishly asked their God for guidance.

"And when we face danger, harm, or even death itself, we take courage from the inspiring examples of the Martyrs of the Revolution and the Heroes of Democracy, and we are comforted by imagining the future destiny of our Country, which we serve by our efforts and our blood. The subject peoples called on God for strength, believing he had all the power and goodness we know is in our Party.

"When we die, we know that we cease to exist, but our memories are preserved by our fellow citizens and our names are inscribed forever in the Hall of Remembrance. The superstitious peoples believed that when they died they would go to live forever with their God in a never-never land called Heaven.

"This is why we are defeating them. We are Realists, Materialists, Objectivists. They are Obstructionists, Reactionaries, Counter-Progressives. What hope does their world of imagination and spirit stand against the steel and blood of our Nation? It is our Country that is the fulfillment of all prior ages and the meaning of History itself."

I raised my hand to ask a question. "Is there anything greater than our Leader?"

He replied, "Only the Party and the State, but these three function as one, for the Party obeys the Leader and accomplishes her will by means of the State. And the Leader acts on the basis of the best possible good for the State. So there is no conflict between them, and they exist in indivisible unity."

Another student raised her hand. "Does the Party ever make a mistake in its decisions and commands?"

"Never," the teacher shook his head. "All dictates of the Leader, and all judgments of the Supreme Council, are absolutely and always true and utterly without error of any kind. Now that does not mean that you or I will necessarily understand the reasoning behind their decisions. Their knowledge and wisdom are far greater than ours; they can see the whole picture, whereas you and I see only our small part. However, you can have absolute trust that the laws and commands issued by official bodies of the State, no matter how confusing or painful they may seem in the short term, will always work for the good of the People as a whole in the long run."

I was reassured by his answers, yet the very suggestion that there might possibly be something greater than the State unsettled me. Until now, I had unquestioningly assumed its superiority and infallibility. Now there was a challenger, however mythical and nonexistent it might be.

Long-suppressed doubts began to surface. For instance, the stars and the earth itself: certainly the Party hadn't made them! Of course not; I'd been told since first grade it was all chance, accident, a colossal beating of astronomical odds against anything existing at all. Nevertheless, I found in myself what I scarcely dared admit even to myself—a yearning to believe. Because if it turned out that the universe was more than just an accident, then maybe I might have been created for a purpose, and my life might have a "meaning" of some sort.

"Ridiculous," my reason replied. "Degenerate romanticist! Objectively, you have no more meaning than a frog or a dog, and they no more than a stone or a germ."

That's all very well, and no doubt true, I responded inwardly, but it still would be nice to have significance in the cosmos, to be able to believe that there really was an all-good and all-powerful being who made everything and watched over it.

I had a similar reaction when visiting the Hall of Remembrance. I went there a couple of times when parents of classmates died. A solemn ceremony was held recalling the character and deeds of the person, a plaque with his or her name was unveiled and fixed high up on a vast wall covered with hundreds of other plaques—and that was it, that was all. Of course it was reasonable, it was sensible—but how much more attractive was the idea of living forever with the God who had created me.

The more I thought about it, the more depressed I became. It wasn't that I believed in any God or non-material power; what upset me was that I didn't have even a possibility of belief open to me. Our Nation, in building its all-powerful State, had eliminated all opposition. By destroying all enemies of the Party, it had obliterated any chance of finding out what they believed. All traces of alternative ideology were erased, all sacred books of the past had been destroyed, all places of worship bulldozed or converted to gymnasiums. There were no options in thought or in life; the Party told us what to believe. All the questions of life were considered political matters, for which the Party had a ready formula. To express dissatisfaction with their doctrine was unheard of—it would bring instant punishment.

So the immovable fact facing me was that, even if God existed—a power greater than the Party, and a personal destiny more lasting than a wall plaque—I had no means to contact it. It was like discovering an old monument with inscriptions written in a dead language; the meaning was totally lost to the present. So any hope of God knowledge was lost to me.

In this gloomy mood, I joined my fellow students in morning assembly. The public reading of our Leader's thoughts seemed boring and hollow. I fretted and fidgeted; my mind tried to escape from the People's Auditorium in which I felt both physically and spiritually confined. But it was useless, hopeless to speculate on any other realm of life. My entire life and eight years of schooling had formed me to be impervious to any higher reality than the State. It not only surrounded me externally, but penetrated me internally, inescapably. My very structures of thought and perception had been laid down on Party principles. Even if a God existed, or any realm of being other than the material one, I would not be able to comprehend it. As a deaf person cannot enter the world of music, so the door to the spirit world was shut to me. Through and through, I was a materialist, who lived and died at the whim and for the glory of my Creator, the State. This was my fate, and there could be nothing more.

Idly I opened the book of patriotic songs, mindlessly joining with my classmates in the familiar refrain:

> O sacred Motherland,
> Thy people's true salvation,
> Only savior of mankind,
> I bow my life to You.
>
> All power and glory are Thine alone,
> All truth and goodness in Thy laws.
> I join with all my fellowmen
> To extol the greatness of Thy domain.

Some students sang it fervently, some monotonously. The smart ones had learned to sing with enthusiasm while making eyes at their girlfriends.

I toyed with the words "O sacred Motherland"—what if it wasn't really sacred, what if only God was sacred? "Thy people's true salvation"—what if God was our salvation, and the Country an impostor? "Only savior of mankind"—well, the whole song could be a lie.

Then it struck me: by changing one word in the song, "Motherland," I could redirect its whole intent, and make it a prayer of worship to the missing deity. "O sacred God, Thy people's true salvation,..." That changed the whole hymn! Then I thought: If, as my teacher had said, a parallel existed between the State and God, so that powers that prior peoples had attributed to God were now assumed by the State, couldn't someone reverse the process and so re-establish contact with the divine Unknown? Suppose all the praise and honor accorded the

Party and our Leader were secretly transferred back to God? Might this not be a means of knowing and reaching it?

Eagerly I leafed through the songbook with new eyes. I read again the familiar songs celebrating the power of the Nation, its goodness, and our need for sacrifice and devotion to it. I knew them all by heart; they were a part of me. They had been the means of my subjection to the State, and now they could become the means of my liberation from it. Merely by changing a word here or there, I could redirect them to that invisible One who loomed above the Party and beyond my small, fragile existence.

Something inside me leaped to life at this revelation. The hopelessness was instantly gone. The incredible thing was that, far from being shut off from communication with the supernatural, I was now aware that I had been unconsciously yet perfectly prepared by my lifelong indoctrination to

Know God.

Double Honor

Let the elders who rule well be considered worthy of double honor (1 Tim 5:17 RSV)

I

Carl Wallace sat at ease on the platform looking out at the congregation. Beside him, waiting his turn to speak, was his good friend John Appleton, professor of New Testament Studies at Reformation Theological Seminary. On the other side of John sat Dr. Tom Edwards, regional superintendent of the United Calvinist Church in America, who also was scheduled to speak briefly. At the podium stood Dr. Ted Hanson, pastor of Marblegate Community Church.

These three men, and indeed the whole assembly, had gathered on Sunday evening in order to pay tribute to Carl upon his retirement from active supervision of the ministry of Marblegate Church. Because he and his wife Marjorie would soon be moving to a retirement community in South Carolina, he had relinquished all his church responsibilities: presiding elder, board member, chairman of the Adult Education committee, and member of numerous other major and minor task forces.

At this moment, Dr. Hanson was recalling in a lighthearted way several anecdotes from his own ten year association with Carl. It was Carl, in fact, as then chairman of the Pastoral Search committee, who had hired him. Carl liked Ted's way of conveying serious truth in a winning and unintimidating manner, without stooping to folksiness or popularity. Carl had often thought that if he had had this same positive personality and friendliness, he himself might have been the pastor of Marblegate, instead of merely a governing elder.

It was not that Carl valued a hearty positive attitude in itself as a qualification for ministry. Personally, he would have preferred a master preacher, an expert exegete, a man who spoke God's Word from the Hebrew and Greek texts. But reality dictated a less desirable pastoral model—reality being a debased culture and an ignorant laity. People wanted little nuggets of Scripture truths suspended in a stream of contemporary allusions and easy applications. "Make the Bible come alive" was how one popular writer put it. "Presumption!" Carl had responded. "It's not the Bible that's dead, but its readers." But it was all to no point. People wanted truth watered down and chopped up and served by a smiling face. Carl had interviewed many pastoral candidates, and Hanson had been the best of the lot, he recalled. He at least had preserved the nuggets of truth, whereas other applicants' sermons were nothing more than the stitching together of a Bible text, a simple moral, and a facile application—all in all, an adult Sunday school lesson. They made

Carl gag. Ted Hanson did better than that. But no one these days, to Carl's deep disappointment, came close to wielding the Word of God as the veritable Sword of the Spirit, fully capable of puncturing the pretensions of this age and of cutting through the self-justifications of modern man. Sadly, the days of the great preachers were past.

After the speeches, Carl knew there would be a presentation of some kind. He wasn't sure what it was, probably a plaque in the Fellowship Hall and a clock to take with them. Marjorie would be invited up on the platform, they would all shake hands, people would clap, he would say a few words of gratitude, and they would all adjourn for cake and coffee. He knew the routine well, since he had so often filled the shoes of one of the laudatory speakers, extolling some departing or deceased deacon or Sunday School teacher. Now, at last, it was his turn.

Nevertheless, no matter what memento they gave him, he knew that the real memorial to his service was not a plaque on the wall, but the very church itself. His association with it stretched way back, long before Dr. Hanson's pastorate. Though man might not realize it, and Carl's modesty would not permit him to mention it, the truth was that the mission of Marblegate Community Church had been the main passion and commitment of Carl's life. To him, his relation to the church, and his increasing responsibilities in it, had been in the nature of a holy calling. Believing that God had put him in these various offices, he had done his utmost in each one of them to fill these roles with dedication and excellence. Carl's first appointment had been deacon of visitation thirty-seven years ago, and he had set up a program which ensured that every visitor, every invalid and shut-in, and every new mother received at least one personal visit. To Carl it hadn't mattered whether the task appointed him was examining a missionary candidate or supervising the overhaul of the restrooms—he had taken on each assignment with the heart of a willing warrior. He had volunteered for the jobs no one else wanted, stepped in when others had quit, made up—out of his own pocket—shortages in church funds for programs that went over budget: Sunday school treats at Easter for preschoolers, Christmas bonuses to the church maintenance staff, the fund to repave the parking lot. Over the years, there had been hundreds of these jobs, large and small, all of them taxing his time, his money, his commitment. Often he had been criticized, sometimes overridden, a few times thanked. But the reactions hadn't mattered to him, not really. Even this final grand send-off failed to move him deeply. Because what Carl had been aiming at all these decades, and what he still looked forward to, indeed the only expectation he had in repayment for all his labors, was a face-to-face meeting in eternity with a smiling Jesus

Christ who would greet him with the words, "Well done, thou good and faithful servant!" This was the secret lodged in Carl's heart, the hidden spring that powered all his devotion to Marblegate Church.

II

Hanson's remarks focused on his acquaintance with Carl and on Carl's contributions to the church during his pastorate. But, in Carl's own view, the definitive battles for the soul of the church and the nature of its witness were fought in previous decades. And it was in these early years, as the culture fell apart, that Carl held Marblegate together.

In the late 1960s there was a strong move in the denomination to liberalize doctrine and modernize church services. This paralleled developments in society at large—the hippie movement, rock music, free love, hallucinogens. Facing the challenges of a hostile youth culture, Carl's generation had split between accommodationists and traditionalists. A certain faction of the church, including the then pastor Rev. Patterson, tried to "relate" to the long-haired, beaded, and sandaled renegades, some of whom had just recently graduated from the prim ranks of the handbell choir. In pursuit of this policy of attempting to win over the youth, numerous alterations were made in the services at Marblegate: a special youth-oriented "happening" was added each week, with guitars in the sanctuary and readings from Che Guevara and Eldridge Cleaver; a newly graduated seminarian with granny glasses and a waist-length pony tail was hired as youth pastor; the Skinner Memorial

Sunday School room was converted to a Saturday night coffeehouse.

In all this, Carl, though at the time a mere deacon, led the forces of counterattack. At church board meetings and in private appointments, he deplored the jettisoning of both biblical truth and conventional decency to appease the demands of a generation of run-amuck teenagers. Rather than endorsing the bizarre habits of dress and absurd beliefs of the young people, the church's duty was to proclaim all the more forcefully the eternal message of the gospel: "Repent and believe!"

A staunch core of opposition clustered around Carl, not only the Old Guard, but a surprising number of more moderate young people and sensible young families. For a long time they could only protest vainly the violations of their sentiments and their faith. But after a couple of years of experimentation and adaptation, it became clear to Pastor Patterson, the majority of the board, and the remaining congregation that the modernizing faction had failed to win over substantial numbers of young people. Instead, membership had declined, costs had increased, church property and facilities had been abused and damaged—and people were tired of having Jesus People in blue jeans and peasant dresses lecture them about the materialism and hypocrisy of the institutional church.

In one stormy business meeting, the orthodox group struck back. Two elders and four deacons resigned, the ponytailed youth minister was fired, and Carl was elected to the board of elders. He had been on it ever since, except for one short period of self-imposed exile. At once, he instituted a thorough purge—youth services were canceled, the Saturday night hangout was recaptured for a Sunday School room (after being thoroughly fumigated), pictures of Huey Newton and the Chicago Seven were trashed.

A few people left, but more people came in, good people, families looking for a solid church with biblical foundations in which to nurture their children. Carl gave it to them—not alone, of course, but he was the acknowledged champion of intelligent conservatism. Far from being a mere faction in the church, Carl's base of support spread throughout the membership. He looked forward to being part of a church with a powerful witness in the community.

Then the tongues-speakers arrived. These were the early days of the charismatic movement. One of the deacons' wives, a rather erratic and unstable lady, had been sucked into this heresy at a conference she'd attended. She returned to infect several other women in the church, and then some of their husbands. Soon a little sect had formed, meeting weekly in a prayer group to practice their glossolalia on each other and to spread the fires of renewal and rebellion.

When Carl first got wind of the existence of an unofficial, unsanctioned faction in the church, his impulse was for immediate suppression of the disruptive elements. Basing his policy on his experience with the hippies, he urged quick and decisive action on the part of the church administration. But there was a difficulty this time. Unlike the earlier situation, when only some young people had been swept up, the charismatic element crossed age and class barriers. Though numerically small, it included members of all Sunday school groups, from teenage through college, adult, and senior adult. The pastor and other elders were leery of enacting a blanket condemnation that would include a few pillars of the church without first getting a definitive word from denominational headquarters that this was indeed a cult.

So Marblegate entered another period of experimentation, much to Carl's dismay. He knew that no good would come of temporizing—the lack of church teaching on the issue just confused ordinary people, and gave the charismatic faction time to strengthen its power base. Eventually, the denomination issued an official rejection of charismatic teaching and practice, a ban that was made more palatable by certain excesses of the charismatics themselves. So the governing board of the church moved decisively to quash the prayer group. But by that time, the damage had been done. Several families left the church; several friendships, some decades long, were permanently ended.

Carl's standing was enhanced because his stance had again been vindicated. Yet it was a credit to him that this made no difference to him. His desire to have his policies enforced was not for reasons of personal pride or status, but for the good of the church and its mission in the community. He knew all along that a house divided against itself could not stand. It was obvious to him. He could not understand why other men in leadership failed to realize so basic a principle. So much grief could have been saved if only they had acknowledged reality early on, instead of giving way to misguided compassion or tolerance.

Though the crisis was past, this was not the end of troubles with enthusiasts. Every couple of years there would be more activity from that quarter: if not over speaking in tongues, then faith healing, prosperity teaching, End-Times fever, prophecies and visions, the healing of memories, and so forth. For a week or a month there would be a little flurry of confusion before stability was restored.

In these subsequent conflagrations, Carl played the role of chief firefighter. He was good at it. He moved quickly to contain the blaze, then politely but firmly extinguished it, through a combination of biblical and denominational teaching and, where necessary, discipline. While he valued the freedom of the individual Christian to differ in matters of faith that were not essential, he drew a firm line at the point where private freedom became public nuisance. People could believe as they wished, but if they practiced their beliefs and imperiled the public peace and mission of the church, he pounced like a hawk. The offenders were duly confronted and reminded of the doctrinal positions of the denomination. Should they refrain from spreading their doctrines, they were welcome to stay; otherwise they were welcome to leave.

Over the years, having weathered numerous contentious disputes, all variations on the same theme, Carl got the reputation of being a hardliner, an arch-traditionalist. He rejected the label, however. Critics and supporters both missed the main issue, in his opinion. To him it was very clear that the main error of the revivalists was the subordination of Scripture to experience. In each case, some ecstatic personal revelation was made the basis for inclusion in the group. This was the essence of their heresy, and indeed of most heresies and cults. He didn't object to tongues-speaking, miracles, or prosperity in themselves, as much as he did to the faulty exegesis promoted by their supporters. "Bubble-heads," he termed them. Or he cited the verse in 2 Timothy 3:6-9:

> For of this sort are they which creep into houses, and lead captive silly women laden with sins, led away with divers lusts, ever learning and never able to come to the knowledge of the truth. . . . their folly shall be manifest unto all men (KJV).

If these people wanted renewal, why did they go elsewhere than to the Word? If they were serious about really knowing God, why didn't they study the Scriptures in the original languages, as he did? Why didn't they discipline their minds instead of indulging their emotions? If they were so devoted to the coming of God's Kingdom, why did they spread division and chaos in the local church?

In time, Carl had become so practiced in apologetics, and so knowledgeable about charismatic beliefs, that he was a truly formidable foe of all innovators. Sometimes the mere warning given by one member to another that Elder Carl did not approve of such and such a teaching was enough to stop the distribution of a book or tape series. No one could defeat him in face-to-face debate. He was methodical, logical, thorough, in all matters of doctrine. His citations of Greek texts and of patristic manuscripts silenced all challengers.

But it would be wrong to conclude, as many chastened opponents did, that he was arrogant and coldhearted. To him, it was a straightforward matter of the logical defense of the faith.

His passionate complaint was that this was every believer's responsibility, not just his own. To that end, Carl had conceived the notion of a layman's course in theology. Why should the pews of American churches be filled with woolly-brained, moronic sheep who became easy prey for every huckster who could afford a radio or TV program? Why not bring theology out of the seminaries and into the churches? Why fight a purely defensive action against doctrinal innovation and syncretism? It was time for the Church Militant to rise and contend for the faith. As Carl saw it, the critical need of our time was an educated and mobilized laity.

III

Pastor Hanson finished his remarks with a strong tribute to Carl and Marjorie's steadfastness. After prolonged applause, John Appleton rose to speak. Carl and John had known each other for over twenty years. Their association began in the days when Carl was still developing his ideas about raising the level of doctrinal knowledge of his congregation. Their relationship had benefited both men and had led each to promotion and prominence in their respective callings.

Carl had discussed his ideas with Rev. Patterson, who had agreed with the concept and then sent him on to talk with denominational superiors. These in turn referred him to the dean of Reformation Seminary, who put him in contact with one of their leading lights, a young New Testament professor. Dr. Appleton was as interested in reaching out beyond campus walls as Carl was in penetrating them. Together they formed a dynamic team, whose major accomplishment over the next five years was the development of a complete course of theological study for Christian laymen, which came to be called Competency in Theological Thinking. Designed to be taken in weekly segments over three years, it would give the interested and motivated believer a basic grounding in the subjects of hermeneutics, biblical languages, biblical and systematic theology, church history, apologetics, and contemporary issues.

This had been a sacrificial labor of love and devotion for both men. Marblegate Community Church had been a test site for each of the units. Carl was gratified at the rise in the level of Christian understanding that he could perceive over the years in the score or so graduates of the program. These were ordinary people, some housewives and blue-collar workers, yet capable of handling an interlinear Bible, expounding the Westminster Catechism, or distinguishing between the objective revelation of God and the subjective apprehension of that revelation. These people, Carl and John both felt, would be the church's main defense against the incursions of fringe groups, and its main offense against the godlessness of the surrounding culture. The course's motto was "You shall know the truth and the truth shall set you free."

This effort had been so successful on a local scale that other Calvinist congregations had adopted it. Indeed, it was fast becoming a denominational standard. One qualification for eldership in any local church was successful completion of the course. There was even an abbreviated one-year course for deacons. The development and distribution of this Competency course was, in Carl's own opinion, the main contribution of his life to God's Kingdom. No doubt it was the reason for tonight's presence of Dr. Edwards from the denominational office. Both Carl and John were looked upon as elders not only in their local churches, but in the denomination itself. Yet again, for Carl, it was not the recognition which made him feel good, but the sense of having been of lasting help to God's work in the world.

IV

As John recounted to the audience the story of the genesis of the theology program, giving pre-eminence to the role of his friend, Carl scanned the faces of the people before him. He recognized nearly every one of them. Many served under him on various boards. Some had studied under him in the Competency program. He knew the names of almost all of them, yet he would have considered few of them his friends. This was not merely a result of his reserved personality. Rather, it was unavoidable, he had realized with reluctance years ago. As with a pastor, the position of elder separated one somewhat from the masses of people. Because he had authority over them, he could not freely associate with them. There was a certain barrier that could not be breached, a certain distance that must be maintained. This was in the nature of all spiritual authority, he had concluded.

Yet there was at least one person in that audience who had never served on a committee with him, never taken a class from him, nor indeed had ever acknowledged his authority. Sitting beside his wife on the front row was his daughter Jennifer, and beside her, her husband Todd. Certainly Carl had not expected her to come! He felt a pang of sorrow in his heart. In all these years (decades, rather) of making decisions for the good of others, of fighting battles on behalf of God's truth, his greatest satisfaction had been the development of the theology course. Everyone present connected his name with this successful program. But very few people, a handful at most, were aware of his greatest defeat, one that crushed his spirit and drained the joy from his accomplishments. Every time he saw her, Carl mourned the loss of his daughter. Not of her life but, to Carl, the greater tragedy of her faith.

While their son Jeff had confessed Christ as a teenager, gone to college, married a Christian girl, and established himself in a career in hotel management, Jennifer had been a disappointment from early teenage years. She had not been one of the wild crowd, but she was shallow, "mush-headed," as Carl characterized her. While she gave lip service to the great doctrines of the church, her vital concerns in her teenage years were nail polish, makeup, and hairstyling.

Carl never understood where his daughter got her preoccupation with such foolishness. Certainly not from her mother: Marjorie was feminine but sensible. He had tolerated Jennifer's flightiness for a while, as just a teenage phase. He kept waiting for her to put down roots, to give some sign of approaching maturity, to evidence some awareness of the serious issues in life, to make her peace with God and take her place as a confessing believer—and for all this he waited in vain. Subsequent controls and restrictions, such as limits on TV viewing and dating, likewise failed to have a positive effect, but served to increase the conflict between them. It got so that he dreaded to look at her, because she seemed intent on violating his standards of modesty and comeliness. Eventually, she had openly defied him by refusing to attend services at Marblegate.

When she left home at eighteen, it was to move in with a truck driver and part-time musician. Carl was devastated—up to this point, everything she had done had been what a Catholic would have considered venial sins, easily forgiven, without great consequences. But this was mortal sin, the irrevocable sundering of spiritual and family relationships. This was a mess that could not readily be untangled.

Beyond his personal grief, Carl suffered in his ministry as well. Citing Titus 1:5-6, Carl confessed that his home was out of order and resigned from the board of elders:

...thou shouldest set in order the things that are wanting, and ordain elders in every city, as I had appointed thee: If any be blameless, the husband of one wife, having faithful children not accused of riot or unruly (KJV).

Carl's departure from leadership caused great consternation in the church, not so much because people thought that he had violated Scripture, but because they had to draft three other people to do all the work he had been doing. It was John Appleton who, at the pastor's urgent request, pulled an exegetical rabbit out of a hat and eventually got Carl to accept reappointment to the eldership. He explained to Carl that the key passage referred only to minor children in the home, and not to grown-up children on their own. By this interpretation, he emphasized, Carl was not only permitted to be an elder but was fully qualified, because he had kept his home in order through almost all of Jennifer's teenage years. Then she had chosen to go her own way, but Carl and Marjorie were not responsible for that. It would be a different matter if they condoned her current live-in relationship or allowed her and her boyfriend to live in their house, but, as it was, they were guiltless.

Gradually, Carl worked through his personal pain, and after a lot of private prayer and a good deal of coaxing by the pastor, he accepted his friend's verdict on the Scripture passage. After a self-imposed six-month sabbatical, he was reinstated as elder, to the relief of the church administration.

But Carl's expectations about his daughter's future were fully vindicated. The young couple moved through successive stages of living together, getting married, having a child, and getting divorced, all within the span of five years. Carl and Marjorie were only remotely involved in any of these events. They attended the wedding, they doted on the grandchild. But Jennifer's visits to her parents were short and seldom, even though she lived in the area. The divorce came without warning, so far as the parents were concerned. Jennifer did not confide in them. When Carl offered her financial help to get back on her feet, she rebuffed him and obtained a secretarial job. Carl and Marjorie never could follow her course over the next several years. Marjorie phoned her once a week and she always said she was fine. She seldom spoke to her father.

So they were shocked when Marjorie learned from an acquaintance at Marblegate that Jennifer was attending Faith Tabernacle across town. The woman had a sister who went there. She knew Jennifer quite well and said Jennifer had been going there regularly for at least six months. Carl didn't know whether this was good news or bad—was their prodigal daughter returning to the fold, or merely continuing her erratic course? Faith Tabernacle was one of those tongues churches Carl detested. He knew of its existence only because some of the more incorrigible charismatics had defected from Marblegate to Faith Tabernacle rather than recant. It pained him to imagine his daughter carrying on with the other unstable people there. On the other hand, when he reflected soberly on the matter, it was quite probable that they were all highly suited to one another. In any case, because Jennifer never brought it up, he and Marjorie never spoke to her about her church attendance.

V

Dr. Appleton finished his speech with warm praise for the man who, by bridging the gap between the man in the pew and the professor in the seminary, had revitalized the educational program of the entire denomination. He sat down, shaking hands with Carl, and Dr. Edwards got up. His presence was evidence of Carl's reputation throughout the Calvinist denomination. Carl was eager for the evening to end. The hard time for him would come later, once he and Marjorie had packed up, moved away, and resettled. What would he do with himself then? He had been involved intimately, nearly every day of the last four decades, with the inner workings of an established congregation. Suddenly he would find himself put out to pasture. It's not that he didn't have things to keep him occupied or interested. His active mind had made plans for a dozen study projects in theology and history. But what outlets would he have for his new insights as well as for his accumulated experience? Carl did not seek personal enrichment for its own sake. Rather his great desire, and the unsolved problem of the future, was to continue to make himself useful.

His thoughts returned to Jennifer. She was his one unsolved problem. Following the discovery of her church affiliation, the next crisis in their relationship had come three months ago when they received a wedding invitation in the mail.

It informed them that Jennifer would be marrying Todd Williams at Faith Tabernacle on September 9th. Carl hit the roof. If Jennifer had previously committed apostasy by leaving the faith, he raged to Marjorie, she was now committing adultery. He read Matthew 5:32 out loud to Marjorie:

> whosoever shall marry her that is divorced committeth adultery (KJV).

"It's plain, isn't it?" he asked.

"Yes," she nodded.

"Then how can any Christian disobey it?"

"I guess they understand it differently than we do."

"Differently? *Differently?* How can you understand a No as a Yes? How can you turn a prohibition into a permission?"

Marjorie tried to calm him down, but he stormed around the house. She finally called Pastor Hanson to come over, which he did. His presence quieted Carl down, without resolving the issue. She finally got him to take one of her sedatives and go to bed.

On his way upstairs, he turned to face both of them.

"I'm not going, Marjorie. I cannot go to that mockery of Christian marriage."

"It's OK, Carl. We don't have to discuss that now. Go and try to rest."

"You can go to it, Marjorie. You're her mother. I understand that. I'm sure God does, too. But I cannot, I will not..." He began to get upset.

Dr. Hanson cut in. "Carl, we'll talk tomorrow. Come over to the office in the morning and we'll pray together. But right now, you need to settle down and get some rest."

Carl sighed and trudged upstairs. When he had gone, Marjorie said quietly, "This really hurts him, Ted. It's tearing him up."

"I know. She's been a real thorn in his flesh for years, hasn't she?"

"It's only because he loves her so dearly, though he never talks about it. And he loves God, too. He thinks that those two loves are in conflict."

"He is a deep man, Marjorie. Very few men would let their love for God intrude on their personal affections and relationships."

"I just hope it doesn't destroy him."

"That's where you come in. Did you hear him? He permitted you to go to the wedding. You're the bridge for him to send his love to Jennifer. She may not recognize it or receive it, but it's just as important that you go as it is that he does not."

The next day, Carl poured out his bewilderment to Ted.

"The Scriptures are clear, aren't they, Ted? I mean, I am not being overly harsh, am I?"

"No, Carl, you know our church's position on the issue of remarriage. No pastor in our denomination may marry a man or woman to a divorced partner. We've always been consistent on that."

"So once again, it's these liberal churches succumbing to the immoral dictates of modern society."

"Yes, it seems that is the popular direction these days—to lower the standards rather than raise them."

"But, Ted, what gets me is, how can you call yourself a church and disobey the plain Word of God? How can you call yourself a pastor and perform a non-biblical sacrament?"

"I don't know, Carl. If I did, maybe we'd rename Marblegate to Hop, Skip, and Jump Fellowship, rip out the pews, and lay down some sawdust."

Carl didn't laugh at Ted's attempt at humor.

"But they're successful, Ted. There are thousands of these fly-by-night spiritual frauds, with millions of followers. It's not just some hole-in-the-wall heresy; it's capturing the mainstream of Christendom."

"And your daughter."

"Yes, and my daughter. I'm not surprised, either. I'm not even angry at her. No, really, I'm not. She's never gotten past spiritual toddlerhood. As such, she is capable of any kind of random spirituality she runs into—from a cult like Jonestown to Catholicism. She doesn't know how to think or reason or believe—she just wanders through life, prey to every wind of doctrine and every false prophet. I pity her, I fear for her, but the ones I'm angry at are the pastors, the wolves in shepherds' clothing, who mislead these people, deceive them, tell them what they want to hear, to their eternal peril. How can they do it, Ted?"

Ted shrugged.

"Is it money, is it ignorance, is it arrogance?" Carl was genuinely confused.

"Probably all of the above," Ted offered. He knew he wasn't answering any of Carl's questions, but he hoped by letting him talk to defuse the personal crisis Carl was going through and let him re-establish some hope for his daughter.

Carl finally decided to write a polite and dispassionate letter to Jennifer, explaining why he could not attend the wedding. He labored for hours over the two pages he eventually handwrote, and asked both Ted and Marjorie to make revisions. After exegeting the Scripture passage and explaining his understanding of the nature of Christian marriage, he closed by stating, somewhat inconsistently but honestly, that he loved her deeply and wished her great happiness in the future. He mailed the letter expecting no response. He received none.

On the day of the wedding, he busied himself in his study while Marjorie wrapped a gift and got dressed. He was tense, lest she pressure him at the last minute to relent. But she knew him well. She stopped at his door on her way out.

"I'm leaving, Carl."

He nodded without looking up.

"I should be home in a couple of hours. There's stew cooking in the crockpot in the kitchen. Just let it simmer."

"OK." He shuffled some papers.

She left quietly. Her own feelings were mixed. She knew Carl was right in his standards. She also knew Jennifer was wrong, as usual. But to her, attendance at the wedding did not signify parental approval or sanction, but merely the acknowledgment of unbreakable family ties. As with a funeral, one did not refuse to attend because of religious differences. Inconsistently, she knew at the same time both that the marriage was a sin and that it was right for her to attend the wedding. She envied her husband, with his clear insight into truth and error. She herself had a far greater tolerance for theological ambiguity.

When she had gone, Carl relaxed. The pressure was off him. He looked at the clock. It was 3:30—the ceremony started at 4:00. He put the papers aside and stared out the window. The weather reflected his depressed mood—it was a mild day, but overcast.

"Lord, why do things like this happen?" he thought idly. "I've always tried to live by your Book, but there are some situations in life that just don't line up."

This was one of them—a classic no-win situation. Nothing he did would satisfy everyone: God, his daughter, his own sense of morality, his role as church elder. He envied his wife, with her own simple, straightforward code of conduct. No one—not even God, he felt sure—would ever reproach her for attending this wedding. And he was glad she was going, he realized, partly because it allowed him the freedom not to go. She got him off the hook. Her attendance symbolized the continuing love and acceptance they offered her; his absence upheld the standards she was flouting.

This was how he'd resolved it in his mind. Yet his heart refused to rest. Carl had no more thoughts to think. It was an insoluble theological problem, and Carl did not believe in insoluble problems. God had an answer for every life situation—Carl believed that. Given enough study of the Bible, personal devotion, counsel with fellow believers, patience, and long-suffering, there was no problem in life that a Christian could not handle in faith. And for the last forty years of his life, Carl had lived accordingly. He had seldom, if ever, knowingly acted contrary to his understanding of God's will in any situation he and Marjorie had faced. It was this that made him an elder, and he upheld this way of life before the entire congregation. This is not to suggest that he was arrogant or self-righteous, merely that he had a clear conscience. But here he could do no right. Here there was no obvious biblical solution. Or there was, but he shrank from it. For the first time, his mind and heart were clearly at war.

He took a deep breath and gave up the struggle. It was twenty to four. He could dress in ten minutes and drive across town in fifteen.

And so he drove there, devoid of joy, devoid of meaning. He went not in faith, but as a man who had no choice and no hope. He went merely to watch, to witness, and not to participate. He went because a love deeper than understanding pulled him there.

He parked two blocks away from the church and walked rapidly to the building. He grimaced at its brashness. At night the words Faith Tabernacle and the pastor's name were illuminated. He repressed his revulsion toward the building and all it represented and pushed on inside. The ceremony had already begun; the bride was at the altar. So he sat quietly and inconspicuously at the back of the church.

Jennifer stood beside a man he did not know, his soon-to-be son-in-law. He saw her white wedding dress and frowned: it was yet another lie. Before them stood the pastor, a young man with slick, sandy hair. Jennifer's seven-year-old son by her first marriage was the ringbearer. He saw his wife on the front row but realized that, mercifully, he recognized no one else there. All of these people were Jennifer's friends from work, her husband's relatives, or Faith Tabernacle church people. It made him feel all the more out of place. He had no connection with her life. His gesture in coming had been futile.

He endured the service, loathing the sermonette extolling the virtues of a Christian marriage. Some day that pastor would have to answer to God for the act he was performing today. And then it was done, and the couple turned to face the congregation.

Jennifer's face glowed as she looked at her friends. He had never seen her so happy—no, never in his memory. It was hard for him to connect the confident, beautiful woman at the front of the church with his predominant image of her as a sullen, resentful teenager. She had grown up from someone he didn't like into someone he didn't know. And now it was too late to reopen the lines of communication between them. They lived in different worlds. The gap was too wide, so wide that now her greatest joy was his greatest sorrow.

The couple began walking down the aisle. Many people in the audience applauded. Carl stood motionless in the back pew, halfway along it, hoping she wouldn't notice him. And she wouldn't have, except that he was by himself, with no one else around him. She was nearly past him when, out of the corner of her eye, she saw him watching her and turned her head toward him.

A look of delighted amazement crossed her face. Dropping her husband's arm, she squeezed along the narrow pew, wedding dress rumpling in the narrow space. Hugging him with one arm, she pressed herself to him in a brief embrace, crushing her bouquet against his jacket.

"Oh, Daddy, I'm so glad you've come!"

She glanced at him with radiant eyes, brushed his cheek with her lips, and then turned and rejoined her husband, who had stopped in surprise at the end of the pew. They continued out the back door of the sanctuary, leaving Carl standing still in astonishment, dazed by the joy of her welcome and the instant realization that he had done the right thing.

He left the church directly, striding wordlessly by the preacher who stood at the door greeting family and friends. He skipped the reception, since he was no good at social functions of any kind, and especially in this case he felt there was nothing to celebrate.

But his daughter's response bewildered him. Such passion, such joy, such love flowed out of her to him in that brief, two-second encounter. She had even dropped her new husband's arm to come over and hug him, an unheard of breach of protocol in any wedding he had ever been to! The spontaneity of her welcome and the evident love she felt for him stirred him deeply and made him very grateful he had gone to the wedding. But what puzzled him most was that her reaction was not the predictable result of a planned moral action on his part. That is, he had not attended her wedding out of any conscious motivation of obedience to God. Far from it! And one of the basic principles of Carl's life, as well as of the Ethics course in the Competency in Theological Thinking program, was that good consequences ensue only from godly actions. Nothing good, in an ultimate sense, is born from haphazard motivations. Yet here was a case of great personal benefit occurring without intentional obedience to divine precept, possibly in defiance of it! He found this extremely troubling, yet his doubts were convincingly overwhelmed by the memory of a joyous face turned to him, an eager embrace, and the scent of flower petals being crushed against his jacket. For all that his mind protested that it had not been God's will for him to go, yet his heart knew that he had just received a rich and special treasure.

Later, Marjorie came home after the reception. She knew Carl had been at the church, both because Jennifer told her at the reception and because she had seen him going down the church steps, rudely pushing past the minister. But she didn't mention it to him, because she knew he didn't want to discuss it with her. She realized what it must have cost him finally to attend. Her heart overflowed. More than just the shared joy of Jennifer's wedding was the foretaste of hope for the healing of her family. To her this was incalculably more important than the theological issues involved. She said nothing to Carl, but, as she passed behind him at the dinner table, she let her hand brush his shoulder and linger there with a gentle squeeze. Carl kept his face bowed over his bowl of stew.

VI

As he looked out over the congregation and saw Jennifer sitting there, Carl understood. Her being there was payback, a gesture of reciprocity for his having attended her wedding. Well, God bless her, it was a decent thing to do. It was another tiny step across the mile-wide chasm that separated them. He would be sure to thank her at the reception. Certainly her return to Marblegate must hold many memories for her—most of them unpleasant. He wondered if perhaps it was almost as hard for her to attend this service as for him to go to the wedding.

Dr. Edwards concluded his address by expressing to Carl the thanks of the entire denomination for his exemplary life and contribution to the church. Now at last the speeches were finished. It was time for the presentation. Marjorie joined him on the platform beside Pastor Hanson at the podium. She was nervous, but Carl was practiced and calm. For him it was the home stretch, the fourth quarter, the ninth inning. Relief was in sight.

Dr. Hanson spoke again. "As many of you know, over the last six months we've been conducting a fundraising campaign to refurbish and expand the Special Ministries Center. This is an area of our church that houses resources and personnel who serve the elderly, young people, and missions. I am pleased to announce that, with the unanimous consent of our board members, this office will be renamed the Wallace Center for Special Ministries, in honor of the extraordinary contributions to our church by these two beloved people."

He held up a wooden sign with the new inscription, as people applauded. Carl nodded his head and smiled, which he hoped would indicate his own acceptance of the honor.

"But," the pastor continued, "we also wanted to give them something tangible to take with them to remember us by." And here he gestured to the church secretary, who came up on stage carrying a two-foot square box. She gave it to Dr. Hanson, who paused for dramatic effect.

"The inscription reads, *To two strong pillars of the church.*" He opened the box and pulled out a block of metal. "We want you to not only take Marblegate with you in memory, but also in replica. This is a scale model of Marblegate Community Church done in pewter by Gerald Atkinson of our congregation, who as most of you know is a professional artist."

He held the model up for all to see, to vigorous applause, then presented it to Carl, who pondered it with due appreciation. Then it was his turn to go to the pulpit.

"On behalf of Marjorie and myself," he began. His remarks flowed smoothly and apparently extemporaneously. Actually, Carl could not tolerate spontaneity in any form and had worked up a small acceptance speech yesterday and memorized it flawlessly last night. His words seemed to express sincere and deep emotion, but Marjorie knew how little this award meant to him.

People applauded, and Carl sat back down. Marjorie returned to her seat in the front pew. The program was ending. Dr. Hanson resumed the pulpit to begin giving instructions about the reception to be held in the Fellowship Hall. Carl sat holding the pewter dust collector in his lap. He noticed that Jennifer was no longer sitting in her place, although her husband was still there. He hoped he would get to speak to her at the reception.

"We hope each of you will join us for coffee and that you will personally express your thanks and congratulations to Carl and Marjorie," Dr. Hanson was saying.

Carl saw his daughter coming back into the sanctuary through the side door, to return to her seat. But she passed by the pew and slowly came up the steps to the platform. She was carrying something carefully in both hands. He turned his head to follow her. She was holding a plate or container of some sort. Was this another presentation? Pastor Hanson faltered in his wrap-up and fell silent. Carl had a premonition of something awful about to happen—after all, Jennifer was so unpredictable. He stiffened in his seat.

Jennifer walked up the carpeted steps with quiet resolution. Dignified and assured, she came directly across the front of the platform toward Carl's chair. There she knelt and set down the towel and full basin of water that she carried. She looked neither at him nor at the speechless and motionless audience.

Only then did Carl realize what she was about to do. In a moment of desperation and terror, he understood and recoiled. Here, in front of all these people, she was going to expose him and their broken relationship. He half-rose in his chair to push her away violently, or to run panic-stricken through the side door, but he sank back, paralyzed before the calm determination of his daughter. She did not hesitate, she did not tremble, she did not ask his permission but, solemn and certain as the judgments of God, she began to untie his shoelaces.

Carl struggled to maintain control. His hands clenched the metal memorial in his lap, the muscles on his jaw and neck stood out, his breathing came short and quick, as of one who is under mortal attack. The embarrassment, the humiliation, the shame were unendurable and unforgivable. Before all these people who had come to honor him, she was stripping bare the family secret, bringing to light the great failure of his life.

He looked desperately at Marjorie. Was she in league with Jennifer? Had she helped set this up? But no—one look at her stricken face, with the knuckles of one hand pressed tightly to her lips, assured him that she had no part in this, that she too suffered with him at his daughter's ludicrous gesture.

She removed his shoes and then his socks. Her movements were not the hasty actions of a servant, but the dignified motions of a priest performing a sacrament. She took a cloth and dipped it in the basin. And then she looked at him for the first time. His eyes darted helplessly from the carpet to the pulpit to his hands, anywhere but at her or the vast sea of witnesses before him. And so she waited. He became aware that she had paused and was looking at him, and he cast a fear-filled glance at her.

She was looking directly at him. He looked away and back again, startled. It was that same vibrant face that had shone on him at her wedding—now turned toward him with a look of piercing clarity, of forthright honesty and tentative mercy. It was a look that accepted him as he was, and yet seemed to expect rebuff and rejection. It was both a statement and a question. She had come to a decision and made her peace—now what about him? Carl again found himself astounded at her. Who was she, this stranger, this daughter of his? She who had torn away from his house in anger and defiance—what had happened to enable her to come back like this, a woman of dignity and spiritual power?

And then she looked down and lifted the cloth from the bowl and washed his feet, firmly and gently, with her head bowed. Just as carefully, she put the cloth aside, dried his feet, and began to replace his socks and shoes.

But Carl was hardly aware of what she was doing. He remained transfixed by the look she had given him. It was both a revelation of who she was and an offering of herself to him. It was as if she were the indulgent parent and he the wayward child, as if she were the one giving forgiveness instead of the one needing it. What was going on here? Wasn't he the aggrieved party? Wasn't he the one who was in the right? Yet there was nothing arrogant in her manner, nothing pretentious or self-righteous.

His act of attending her wedding had prompted an unexpected reaction from Jennifer. Now her own radical submission called for some response from him. But what response could he make and still retain control? His heart sought desperately to break the limits set on it by his past role of authority over her, his identity as a parent and elder. His daughter had taken the initiative to erase the entire record of misdeeds and hurt feelings that stood between them, and she was now giving him an open door to her heart. He had only to stretch forth his hand in some simple gesture of acknowledgment, to touch her hair or shoulder. Just a touch, and yet he held back: what would all these people think if he broke down and embraced her in front of them all?

Jennifer finished tying his shoes, then raised herself to lightly kiss him on the cheek. Gathering the cloth and basin, she got up and walked slowly down the steps, like a bride processing down the aisle, leaving behind her a stunned and humbled man, who for the first time in his life had been confronted with the cost of being born again.

Of Wind and Wave

When I first saw them that early fall day, they were already in the middle of the lake, in a small rowboat, heading for the opposite shore; he pulling on the oars steadily, rhythmically, she sitting rigidly in the stern, back to me, hands clenching the seat. He was at ease on the water, confident, skilled in maneuvering the small craft, seldom glancing over his shoulder to correct their course. She seemed diffident, timid, doubtful, as if anticipating a large wave would suddenly upset them, or a hole open in the bottom of the boat and they sink at once like a stone.

They were alone on the water, bound perhaps for a picnic together among the trees and foothills across from me. It was a small lake, only a few hundred yards in length. They looked to me like a water bug skimming the surface of a large puddle.

I sat and watched, not intending to intrude on their privacy, nor wanting them to infringe on mine. I had been following a trail leading through marshland and winding among pools and streams that fed this lake. This was a place to rest and think and listen. I had come here seeking peace and vision and that sense of replenishment that comes only when one forsakes for a while all human contact.

Somewhere in this scene, in the interaction of trees and wind and sky and water, yes, and even that rowboat, there was a harmony and meaning in which I hungered to participate. If it had been a motorboat, I would have been offended. If they had brought a radio, the peace would have been destroyed. They were talking, or at least he was speaking to her. I couldn't hear his words, but the effect of them was that she slowly relaxed. By the time they neared the far shore, her hands were off the seat and folded in her lap, and she moved gently in time with the boat's motion. She was no longer afraid.

My eyes closed, my thoughts drifted back to my own life, my own problems—the very things I'd come to get away from. Such a contrast between this peaceful setting and daily life, a place where things certainly were not in order. Events and people succeeded each other haphazardly. I felt that it was up to me to fit them together in some meaningful pattern: cohesive, purposeful, intelligible—this is The Story of My Life. Several scripts were running simultaneously, several subplots being acted out at one time, but with no hint of convergence. It was as if someone had dumped the contents of four different jigsaw puzzles together and tried to come up with one picture. The harder I worked at it, the less sense it made.

The breeze brushed my face. I had dozed off for a few minutes. The wind rippled the water's surface, breaking the sun's light into fragments. It pushed a few wispy clouds across the sky and rustled the leaves of the trees. The green border of the lake came alive, swaying back and forth, waving to me. I suddenly realized how flat and dull this whole panorama would be without the gentle force of the wind moving on it—land and water a monotonous tableau beneath a monochrome sky. All these elements drew their life, their visual vitality, from its invisible presence. Yes, and it was the wind that had blown the woman's hair when I first saw her in the boat . . . the boat! Where was it now? I looked for it, but it had vanished.

What? That was impossible. I stood up, scanning the far shore. They should have reached land by now, but there was no sign of man, woman, or boat. The same scene that had brought me peace and enjoyment now filled me with alarm. But even if the worst had happened—the boat capsizing—there would have been some trace of their accident. I hurried down to the shore and ran along it in the direction they had been going. It would take only a few minutes to reach the head of the lake.

I ran anxiously, the mood of the morning thoroughly shattered, my quiet meditation replaced by dread and foreboding. Out of breath, I neared the far side of the lake, and only as I came to the very corner of it did I see the channel. It was a narrow waterway, a canal winding between the banks, hidden from view by a rise of land on the near side. What I had assumed to be a self-contained lake was, in fact, connected to something else.

The couple must have followed this narrow course, at once disappearing from my view. Now I gave chase, discreetly so as not to take them unawares, but determinedly. The fear was gone; I felt myself both an explorer and a detective. Near the water's edge, I clambered over fallen trees and around rock barricades. This was a more difficult passage, but not as long as the lake shore. Soon the channel began to broaden and turn. A little further and it opened out onto . . . another lake! So what I had assumed to be the far shore of the lake I had left was in reality, I could see now, a headland separating these two bodies of water. The former was but an inlet, a sheltered cove, of the one whose banks I now stood on.

To my left was a long curving shoreline, and a rock promontory thrusting into the water. To my right, across the mouth of the channel beside me, lay the abrupt rise of the headland, and beyond that, hills framing the water and receding into the distance. The immensity of this vision pressed in on me with all the greater intensity after the cramped view I'd had while stumbling along the narrow canal.

And before me, there they were at last!—fifty yards offshore, my friends, though I had never met them. But so they were, true friends nonetheless. He was rowing as he had when I'd first seen them, confidently, methodically. Even though the waves were larger here, the power of the water so much greater, he seemed just as assured as he had been on the surface of the inlet. But she—ah, she'd lost her confidence, she too was as I remembered her at first: clutching the seat, sitting straight up, her body fighting the boat's movement. I laughed with relief. They were all right after all. They really were, though she didn't believe it. I could see he was talking to her again. In time she would relax. But for now she grasped the boat with both hands and stared fearfully at their destination.

I followed her gaze out toward the far shore but could see little because I was standing so low at the water's edge. So I climbed the rocky outcropping along a rough and steep path that took me a good quarter of an hour. From that height, shielding my eyes, I looked out past their tiny craft, out past the wind-animated waves, in the direction they were going. And then I felt her fear, compounded with my own astonishment, for as far as I could see, there was nothing, nothing—nothing at all but the curve of the earth and the blue of an infinite sky.

Star Trek

As a planet around a distant sun, so I circle this star. It ever glows as the center of the revolving speckled darkness behind it. Gradually, I realize that it controls my own spiral through the void. It tugs at me, but I resist and run away from it. Yet it keeps pulling me and will not let me fly off to eternal directionless flight.

So faint, so invisible the ties, yet so tenacious! This brilliant dot slowly grows, so that I cease to lose it among its rivals in my universe. It is there, still holding me, still drawing me in. Yet I dodge and run in a crazy orbit, sometimes veering dangerously close, so that the whole sky fills with its fire, sometimes turning my back on it and plunging into the frigid vacuum of the outer darkness.

Watch out! That last pass was frightfully near, so that I felt the tremendous explosions scatter the darkness for millions of miles in every direction. The heat melts away the dross within me, transforming my very substance. The pull of gravity upon me is so great that I begin to break apart. I can no longer breathe, no longer resist. Dissolution will be total long before impact.

Two jets of fire reach out to engulf me. They shape themselves into arms, with open hands. I look up in wonder. It is the Lord.

www.ingramcontent.com/pod-product-compliance
Lightning Source LLC
Chambersburg PA
CBHW072157070526
44585CB00015B/1188